WITH

D0056829

A CONGRESS OF WONDERS

ALSO BY ED MCCLANAHAN

The Natural Man

Famous People I Have Known

CONGRESS

of

WONDERS

ED McCLANAHAN

COUNTERPOINT
WASHINGTON, D.C.

Portions of this book appeared, in different form, in *Esquire*,
The Journal of Kentucky Studies, *Kentucky Renaissance*, *Per Se*,
Pine Mountain Sand and Gravel, *Place Magazine*, and *Stanford
Short Stories 1964*. The author also gratefully acknowledges
a Wallace E. Stegner Fellowship in Creative Writing at
Stanford University, two Yaddo Foundation fellowships,
and the Kentucky Arts Council's Al Smith Fellowship,
all of which supported the writing of these stories.

Library of Congress Catalog Card Number: 96-84003

ISBN 1-887178-12-0

FIRST PRINTING

Book design by David Bullen
Composition by Wilsted & Taylor

Printed in the United States of America on acid-free paper
that meets the American National Standards Institute
Z39-48 Standard.

COUNTERPOINT
P.O. Box 65793
Washington, D.C. 20035-5793

Distributed by Publishers Group West

This one is for the boys: "Juanita and the Frog Prince" for Wendell and Gurney, from whom I boosted all the good stuff; "The Congress of Wonders" for Nedro, pal o' my youth, true in my dotage; "Finch's Song" for KC, the Mayor of Skylonda. And the whole works is for my main men, Jess and Bill.

 # Contents

"To a new world
of gods and monsters!"

Dr. Prætorious, the mad scientist in
Bride of Frankenstein, proposing a toast

JUANITA

and the

FROG

PRINCE

WELCOME TO BURDOCK COUNTY, hails the peeling roadside billboard out at the county line, THE ASPARAGUS BED OF THE COMMONWEALTH.

Not that anyone in Burdock County actually *grows* asparagus in any noteworthy quantity; we're in tobacco country here, and asparagus makes, at best, an indifferent smoke. It's rather that the noble vegetable is reputed to insist upon the choice spot in the garden for itself, and civic-minded Burdock Countians like to suppose they're at least as discriminating as a stalk of asparagus.

At what is purported to be at once the highest point of ground and the exact geographical center of the county, the Burdock County courthouse, an ash-gray pile of colonnaded, crenellated stucco, bulks exceeding large, with the village of Needmore, nine hundred citizens strong, abjectly huddled round it, and the wrinkled hills and dales of Burdock County tumbling off to the four horizons like a vast unmade bed. Until recently, the predominant color in this great rumpled patchwork vista would have been green— the bosky verdure of woods and thickets, the paler shades of meadows and cornfields and tobacco patches—but the harvest season's over now, and the first frost has come and gone; and on this day—a certain fine late October Sunday afternoon in 1941—the orange and dun and russet hues of autumn are in the ascendancy.

Atop the courthouse, that imposing eyesore, is situated yet another imposing eyesore: a bulbous, beehive-shaped cupola with four clock faces the size of mill wheels, each asserting with all the authority of its hugeness four entirely different times of day. Two sides of the clock have, in fact, long since concluded that being right twice a day is better than never being right at all and have taken their stands at, respectively, 9:14 and 7:26. The remaining pair toil on, not in tandem but quite independently, one gaining several seconds every hour, the other just as resolutely losing them. There is, moreover, a bell in the clock tower that has a timetable all its own and is liable to toll midnight at three in the morning and noon at suppertime. The dedicated public servants in the courthouse learned long ago to ignore altogether the two broken clocks and the bell and to come to work by the slow clock and knock off by the fast one. They regard their singular timepiece as a labor-saving device and treasure it accordingly.

". . . that the said defendant Luther Jukes, aka Two-Nose Jukes, in the village of Pinhook in the county of Burdock, on the twenty-third day of August, A.D. 1941, and before the finding of

this indictment, did unlawfully, feloniously, and maliciously, with force and arms, deposit at, in, and near a doorway on a porch being that of the Bludgins Texaco Station and Garage, owned and operated by Lonzo W. Bludgins, aka Lugnut Bludgins, and the place where Lonzo W. Bludgins was then employed and did work, a package consisting of a Dutch Masters cigar box enclosing a deadly weapon, to wit: a weight bomb loaded with nitroglycerin, batteries, nuts and bolts, nails, hinges, and similar hard, egregious, and explosive substances, the said Luther Jukes, with the felonious and malicious intent then and there to kill, wound, and injure the said Lonzo W. Bludgins, a human being, by means of said deposit, and the said Lonzo W. Bludgins not then knowing that the said package contained nitroglycerin and/or explosive substances did place his hand upon it and that, as a result thereof, the said package did explode, thereby wounding the said Lonzo W. Bludgins in, about, and upon various portions of his anatomy, body, and person, and from which shooting, explosion, and wounding, death did forthwith occur . . ."

The Burdock County jail occupies the entire northwest corner of the courthouse grounds and complements its larger sister by presenting to the mercantile establishments across the street an equally grim visage, rendered in the same ashy stucco complexion. The structure weds a stolid gray bungalow of inconsolably gloomy aspect—here reside the duly elected county jailer, currently Dutch Louderback, and his family—to a miniature Bastille, replete with barred embrasures and steel shutters and little fake oriels and battlements. This edifice squats, ogreish and ominous, against the bungalow's posterior and is not infrequently the temporary residence of one or another—or several—of the jailer's in-laws, the Souseleys, who tend to drink a little.

In recent weeks, however, there has languished in the jail's coziest—in terms of elbow room—and most secluded cell a sojourner vastly more distinguished than the usual assortment of weekending Souseleys and other small-time miscreants, misanthropes, and misfits. Indeed, the present occupant of Jailer Louderback's dank little accommodation has distinguished himself in all three of those areas of endeavor: in miscreancy by having summarily dispatched to a better world the said Lugnut W. Bludgins by means of the said infernal device; in misanthropy by cordially despising the entire human race and everyone in it; and in misfittedness by looking at the world from behind a physiognomy that boasts, among sundry other remarkable features, precisely twice the regulation number of noses—which is to say, two. Noses.

By way of description—to get it over with—let's just say that the two olfactory organs are situated side by side, that they share a common nostril (for a grand total of three), and that neither is of anything remotely approaching noble stamp. Above this distinctive bifurcation, its proprietor's dark eyes glitter with malign intelligence; below it, due to some structural facial anomaly attendant upon the excess of noses, his lips are twisted into a crooked grimace, the fixed, malevolent parody of a grin. His complexion is of a strange gray-green cast, not unlike that of the jail itself, a condition that has given rise to speculation that he was sired by a Chinee, or a Hindoo, or a Portagee, or even, in the opinion of two or three local Flash Gordon fans, a Martian or a Moonman. And for good measure, he is as bowlegged as a terrapin, the result of a childhood bout with rickets, and his ears stand out from his head like a Ford coupe with both doors open.

The proper name of this understandably irritable personage is Luther Jukes, but human nature being what it is, all his days he has been called—though rarely to his ill-conditioned face—"Two-Nose," a soubriquet that, carelessly employed, cost the late Lugnut Bludgins his very life. Yet even that extreme measure hasn't had the desired effect, for now, as he awaits trial, certain conviction, and life without parole, Two-Nose Jukes owns the most celebrated name in Burdock County.

Juanita Sparks, hoosegow scullery maid and orphaned niece of the jailer's wife, stands at the jail-yard clothesline with a mouthful of clothespins and an armful of wet convict underwear. She has felt like s-h-i-t all this livelong day, ever since she woke up with morning sickness for the fifth time in a row.

When she thinks about the way those old boys, Warren Harding Skidmore and Sharky Vance and Dime Logan and them, have been a-wallering her in the backseat of Warren Harding's car lately, hopping all over her like fleas on a hog-lot dog, she's about decided that this old s-e-x ain't half what it's cracked up to be.

And now it's a regular old boogeyman she's got on her hands, a downright murderer, that two-nosed thing, that Jukes. Juanita can't hardly bear to look at him herself; her eyes land on his forehead every time and then just slide off his face like two fried eggs out of a skillet. But one time she came in to mop when he was on his bunk, asleep, so for the first time she could stand there and just look and look at him, staring at him with all the eyes in her head, till all at once his own eyes popped open, and she seen that he was wide awake, grinning at her as though they shared some awful secret.

Juanita didn't say a word, she just grabbed her mop and fell to mopping like she was killing snakes. But ever since, whenever she feels him looking at her, she knows that if she looks back that terrible grin lies waiting for her, just like a boogeyman in the dark.

Here lately, though, whenever there's nobody else around, he's been trying to talk to her, saying the strangest things. Like one morning, as she was mopping along in front of his cell, he'd said, right out of the blue, "Maud Muller on a summer's day, raked the meadow sweet with hay."

Don't you know the difference between a rake and a mop? Juanita had thought. But she didn't say a word.

Another time, he said, "I ain't nowhere near as bad as people says I am. Since when was genius found respectable?"

Only a day or two ago, just as she was finishing up the corridor, he'd sung out, "No one is so accursed by fate, No one so utterly desolate, But some heart, though unknown, Responds unto his own. You'd like me, sister, if you just knowed me better!"

Juanita never could make heads nor tails out of it herself; she always just kept on mopping and pretended like she hadn't heard him. Still, the words stayed with her, even the big ones, and she turned them over and over in her mind, wondering about them.

But she did recognize the poem about Maud What's-her-name, from Miss Gantley's English class. It told a story about this Maud, which was a farm girl that loved a judge which come riding up on a big horse. It was the one that ended, "For of all sad words of tongue or pen"—to this day, Juanita can't hardly think about it without getting a tear in her eye—"the saddest are these: 'It might have been!' "

Wearily, Juanita picks up her empty basket and heads back to the jail basement for another load, wondering what in the Lord's name ever took ahold of her to make her quit school and go into cleaning up after a bunch of old jailbirds anyhow. Old drunkerts a-puking and dirtying theirselfs and carrying on all night long about the rats and snakes and spiders that can't nobody see but them. She don't care if most of them *is* her own mommy's kin, you just don't meet your finer high uppity-up quality of people in a jail.

If anybody in Burdock County should've known better than to address Luther Jukes as "Two-Nose," Lugnut Bludgins was the man, considering that he had made the same mistake more than twenty years before, when they were schoolmates, and had received a brickbat to the side of the head in return for the compliment. But Lugnut was nothing if not a nincompoop—indeed, it might be argued that he was nothing *but* a nincompoop—and so when he saw Luther, with a ragged hobo bedroll on his shoulder, walking through Pinhook for the first time in years, he greeted him, with even less wisdom than wit, as follows:

"Well, look who's back! Where you been, Luther Two-Nose, Hollywood?"

Where Luther had been lately, as it happened, was in the state penitentiary in Missouri, serving eighteen months for assault with intent to kill a deputy sheriff who had unburdened himself of a similar jocularity. His cellmate there had been an accomplished safecracker with a pedagogical bent, and Luther had proved an apt apprentice. And so it came to pass that on the very night of Lugnut's little indiscretion, a certain resourceful party broke into a storage shed at the county highway department and made off with a quantity of nitroglycerin and dynamite caps. The following morning, Lugnut Bludgins received the transmogrifying parcel, and instantly was no more.

There had been several witnesses to Lugnut's ill-advised pleasantry of the day before, and within hours Luther Jukes was lodged in the county jail, where he has abided ever since. His trial is now just weeks away, yet he steadfastly refuses even to discuss his case with the attorney appointed to defend him.

"There's two sides to any story," he told the attorney, "and there's two sides to this one. My side is, some people is just too goddamn dumb to live."

Otherwise—except for those inscrutable musings he's shared with Juanita—the only person he's talked to at any length is his grandmother, a dreadful old harridan named Sallie Jukes, who made her way to town on foot just once to visit him at the window of his cell, where they conferred through the bars in hisses and whispers, like hostile serpents.

———

Two-Nose Jukes is a local product— or, more accurately, a local by-product. He is the fatherless issue of the wayward daughter of the irascible, gimlet-eyed old Sallie Jukes, who has lived since time immemorial on Morgadore Creek, a couple of miles down the road from Pinhook, in two or three rooms of a great, gloomy old log house that has been otherwise abandoned and in ruins for generations.

The widow Jukes lost her husband aeons ago to a serving of her own home-canned green beans, delicately seasoned, legend has it, with a pinch of rat poison and offered at supper on the very day that she discovered him in the barn fraternizing a bit too intimately with the livestock.

The daughter—"Sweaty Betty," as she was known affectionately by her admirers—eventually made herself charming to every unfettered male in the neighborhood, perhaps to ensure that Sallie's woodpile would keep growing even during the longest winter. Betty ran off with a passing tramp around the start of the First World War, urged on by the heartfelt curses of her abandoned parent, and didn't reappear until the early twenties, when a neighbor of old Sallie's recognized her one wintry day walking down the road in the direction of her mother's home, with a child, muffled to the eyeballs against the bitter cold, trudging at her side. A few hours later the neighbor saw her pass again, alone, never to return.

Now these were dark and ignorant times, long before the land had been enlightened by yet another world war, and Sallie Jukes's uncomely visage, her habit of muttering angrily under her breath about male perfidy and falseness, and especially her line of work—she sewed shrouds and laid out bodies for a Pinhook mortician—had long fostered among her neighbors the suspicion that she had access to sinister forces and was up to no good. The neighbors believed, or professed to believe, that she was surreptitiously fixing them with the Evil Eye, predisposing them to stub a toe or catch a thumb in the rattrap or drop the brand-new Monkey Ward catalog down the privy. "Bad-Cess Sallie Jukes," she was called. A glance from her could sour milk, it was said, or start a toothache, or induce a cake to fall. Over the years, the sheer volume of mischief attributed to Bad-Cess Sallie Jukes would have put a moderate natural catastrophe to shame.

Sallie augmented her shroud money by gathering herbs, roots, and berries for the manufacture of a line of soothing balms and purgative nostrums, which she concocted in her famous kitchen and peddled door to door. Her clientele bought her wares not out of any abiding confidence in their curative powers but rather as talismans to ward off the venerable apothecary's pernicious influence.

And when she began turning up on their doorsteps with her own personal little hobgoblin at her side, who stood there grinning as though he were enjoying some unspeakable private joke, her fame was much enhanced, and business at her roving pharmacy increased twofold in a single season.

There's too many squirrels in that family tree, people told each other knowingly—there's a dead cat on the line somewheres. In the more benighted reaches of the county, where darkness and superstition still hadn't given way to progress, there was general agreement that those curses the old woman had hurled after her departing daughter had devolved upon the child, surely to Sallie's infinite satisfaction.

In due course, an ad hoc committee of local eminences determined that in the interest of preserving the scenic beauty of Burdock County, an effort should be made to persuade old Sallie to turn her unsightly ward over to the Commonwealth, trusting that august body to find a spot for him in some dank corner of one of its more remote institutions. To advance their proposal, they dispatched a delegation of three—led, perhaps significantly, by Amos Bludgins, father of the ill-fated Lugnut, accompanied by a neighboring farmer and Pinhook's only barber, in whose shop the plan was hatched.

But Sallie, cradling her late husband's rusty double-barreled twelve-gauge in her arms, received them in her dooryard, the reputed Imp of Satan peeking out from behind her voluminous skirts, grinning hospitably, as if he'd like nothing better than to dash out and bite the company on its several ankles.

"Git," the old woman welcomed them.

"Now, Mother Jukes," Amos began, removing his hat and gamely stepping forward, "we just . . ."

Sallie brought the shotgun to her shoulder, sighted down the barrel at the balding Bludgins pate, and said, in a voice as bleak as ashes, "How'd you like me t' jump yore head off?"

"Now, Miss Sallie, now," said Amos, backpedaling a step, "we're good Christians, we wouldn't want to get mixed up in nothing like that."

Sallie drew back a firing hammer with her thumb. "Git, then," she said. "Hesh up and git."

The committee adjourned itself on the spot and retired in disarray. But at the end of the lane, Amos Bludgins did look back long enough to see old Sallie point the shotgun to the sky and fire it, first one barrel then the other, while the bandy-legged Imp of Satan danced about her with antic glee.

Within the ensuing month, lightning struck the farmer's henhouse and fricasseed his entire flock of leghorns, and the barber, in an absentminded moment, snipped off the tip of Amos Bludgin's earlobe and had to close up shop and leave town in disgrace. Clearly, it did not pay to mess with Bad-Cess Sallie Jukes.

In due time, the county prevailed upon Sallie to send the boy to school, where he proved, to universal astonishment, to be a remarkably quick study, picking up the three R's so handily, by some mysterious osmotic process, that it almost seemed to his teachers that the skills were already there inside his ugly little head, a wellspring just waiting to be tapped. His capacities, the teachers sensed uneasily, went beyond mere intelligence into the realm of the unnatural, as though he knew more than they did.

In all other respects he turned out to be as intractable and truculent as old Sallie herself. Small for his age, he was nonetheless as tough as toenails and would fight at the drop of an insult or the merest flicker of a disparaging stare, with whatever weaponry came to hand, rock or stick or clawhammer or coal scuttle, all the while grinning like a frolicsome gargoyle. On more than one occasion, he augmented his education by kicking teachers in the shins. It was even rumored that when cornered, he had the power to regurgitate upon his enemies at will, as certain poisonous toads are said to do.

So his acquirements did little to enhance his popularity, and when he failed to show up for the fourth grade, there was rejoicing at Pinhook Elementary, and no one gave the first thought to calling out the truant officer.

In the basement, standing at the washing machine running coveralls through the wringer, Juanita can hear the crazy old one-legged street preacher, the one they call Baloney Jones, stumping on his crutches up and down the steel-plated floor between the cells and the drunk tank, squawking at the drunks the way he does every Sunday afternoon, talking long distance to Jesus on the toy telephone he carries around his neck, telling him what a viper's nest of sinners Brother Baloney finds himself among today—just as if Jesus didn't know all that already, or why would they be in jail in the first place?

It was that Miss Gantley, Juanita reminds herself grimly as she feeds another pair of coveralls to the wringer, Miss Gantley the eighth-grade homeroom teacher, which was just plain j-e-double-l-o-u-s when Juanita came back for her second year in eighth grade bigger in the bustline than little old puny-tits Miss Gantley her own self, and when Sharky Vance tried to feel of them in the cloakroom and she kicked him in his textacles the way her own daddy told her to before he went and died of sclerosis of the liver, Miss Gantley sent her—Juanita!—to the office with a note that said *she* was a bad influent!

So Juanita seen right then and there whichaway the land laid, and from then on she just let Warren Harding and Sharky and Dime and them play with her bustesses any old time she felt like it. Which that turned out to be not near as often as *they* felt like it, them boys, and it wadn't long till they'd about drove that old s-h-i-t into the ground.

So she quit school in the ninth grade, the day she turned sixteen, and her Uncle Dutch got her on with the county, doing the laundry and swabbing up after the jailbirds, and now she's went and got herself pragnent, which that is why—watching the last pair of coveralls issue from the wringer, as flat and inky blue as the indigo shadow of the man who'd worn them—which that is just exactly why Juanita wishes with all her heart that little Miss Puny-Tits Gantley had went and got the big bustesses instead of her. It'd serve her right, the old b-i-c-t-h.

"Now listen to me, O my honeys!" Juanita hears Brother Jones implore his little flock as she lugs her wash basket up the cellar stairs. "Sinnin' is like drinkin' outta the spittoon, don't you see! For it's all in one piece, O my honeys, and oncet you start, you can't quit till you've drunk 'er dry!"

Lord, Lord, Juanita sighs. Like s-h-i-t warmed over, that's exactly how she feels.

_____

In his early manhood, young Luther Jukes took up the most solitary trade available: he became a woodsman, a hunter, a very Nimrod stalking the countryside with his grandfather's ancient shotgun on his shoulder and a pack of vicious, half-starved curs surging all about him. Thus did he keep old Sallie's stubbled chin well greased with varmint drippings.

Later, during the second half of the 1930s, Luther left the old woman to her mutterings and set forth to make his way in, of all things, the religion game, taking to the road as the disciple—or, if you please, accomplice—of a barnstorming reprobate tent preacher who billed himself as the Right Reverend P. C. Rexroat, D.D., Archbishop of the Canvas Cathedral of the Resurrection, the Light, the Divine Afflatus, and the Main Chance.

The archbishop, as it happened, had been casting about for a square-up act, an attraction rather less ephemeral than the Holy Spirit to entice flocks of potential Lambs of God into the Canvas Cathedral for a good fleecing. When, in his travels, he heard reports of the Burdock County prodigy, he made a pilgrimage to Pinhook at the earliest opportunity.

Like the Bludgins committee before him, he was obliged

to stand in Sallie's dooryard and pay his compliments down the twin barrels of the shotgun—wielded this time by young Luther, while the old woman stood by with a pitchfork at the ready. But unlike his predecessors, Reverend Rexroat never even flinched—for he was sustained not only by his faith in the Creator of Us All (of which the theologian actually possessed the minimum, though he did not scruple to invoke Him at every opportunity) but also by his complete confidence in a far more reliable certitude, that of irreducible human avarice.

"Madam," he began, in a voice like oil on troubled waters, "our Creator enjoins us against hiding our light beneath a bushel. This lad"—he indicated Luther with a bow—"is a national treasure. It is our sacred duty to exploit that treasure in the service of the Lord."

"Git," came the response, predictably. It was accompanied by a menacing feint with the pitchfork.

"My good woman, kindly desist until you've heard me out. It is true that the Lord has put us in this vale of tears that we might earn our way into his kingdom by our good works, yes, indeed. But in the meantime, he also wishes us to do *well*, you see, to reap the rewards of *this* world for our labors in his vineyard. This young man's face"—the reverend struggled to suppress a shudder at the thought—"could be our fortune. In short, madam, what would you say to, ah, eight dollars a week, direct to you via the U.S. mail?"

"If you would've said ten," Sallie allowed, lowering the pitchfork ever so slightly, "I mighta heered you better."

"Ten it is," the reverend conceded. "I meant to say ten."

"And keep?"

"Ten and keep," he sighed.

"Luther," said the old woman, "put that shotgun down and go fetch this preacher a drink of water. He's got some talkin' to do."

———

Monday mornings are the worst, as far as Juanita is concerned. They turn loose all the drunks on Sunday evening, so her first job of a Monday is to hose down the drunk tank and swab it out, which is enough right there to make a person ashamed of being a Souseley.

And if that's not bad enough, when Juanita come out of the johnny this morning after she had her morning sickness, she noticed her Aunt Jimmie looking at her real funny, and then Aunt Jimmie looked over at Uncle Dutch and kind of rolled her eyes, like, and Juanita just *knew* they smelt a rat somewheres.

So later on, when they're eating breakfast, she leaves off her wet-mopping and sneaks down the hall to the kitchen door, where she can listen in on them.

"Do you reckon," Aunt Jimmie is saying, "that a man could have got to that child?"

"Well," says Uncle Dutch, sucking his teeth, "a good big boy coulda done it."

Then Aunt Jimmie sets down her coffee cup so hard Juanita can hear it smack the table, and says she's got half a mind to march the girl right straight down the street to Dr. Winnaberry's office. "We run a nice Christian jail here," Aunt Jimmie declares. "If Doc Winnaberry was to say the little snip's in trouble, I'd send her back to the homeplace so fast it'd make her nose bleed. That'd learn her not to go around with her titties stuck out!"

"Some of them says she's runnin' after that Skidmore," Dutch offers. "Maybe he'll marry her."

"Pshaw!" Jimmie snorts. "That worthless thing ain't gonna marry nobody, and there ain't one single Souseley that's man enough to make him!"

Almost reeling, Juanita turns and tiptoes away, holding her breath to choke off a sob. And it is just at this most dismal moment that she remembers something her girlfriend Harletta Porch, who lives in Pinhook, once told her about Bad-Cess Sallie Jukes.

In the gloomiest chamber of the dark inside Juanita's head, a little light comes on. Suddenly she knows what she must do: she has to talk to Luther Jukes.

Philander Cosmo Rexroat was a sky-grifter of the old school. In the fair-weather seasons, he plied the back roads in an ancient LaSalle sedan the size of a locomotive, towing a ramshackle house trailer with a stubby crucifix mounted atop it, like an overgrown sarcophagus. The cross bore on either side the modest legend:

$$
\begin{array}{ccccccc}
 & & R & & & & \\
 & & E & & & & \\
 & & X & & & & \\
R & E & X & R & O & A & T \\
 & & O & & & & \\
 & & A & & & & \\
 & & T & & & & \\
\end{array}
$$

His plan, as Rexroat disclosed it to old Sallie, was to effect the instant metamorphosis of young Luther Jukes into a former heathen whom His Eminence, through the sheer vigor of his enunciation of the Word, had brought to his knees at the feet of the Lord during the latest Canvas Cathedral missionary expedition to the godless Orient.

To that purpose, Rexroat, after studying his subject's dingy, leaden complexion for as long as he could bear it, uttered an "Aha!" and plunged into the trailer. A good deal of noisy, expletive-punctuated rummaging ensued, until he finally emerged with an old gray flannel bathrobe, a pair of worn Mexican huaraches with tire-tread soles, a white chiffon window curtain with a fringe of little yarn snowballs, and an extra-wide, hand-painted, gravy-embellished necktie depicting a bucolic autumn scene, complete with falling leaves, pumpkins, Thanksgiving turkeys, and tiny square dancers.

After Luther had stripped to his drawers and donned the flannel caftan and the sandals, the reverend, averting his eyes from his new protégé's cloven mug as best he could, fashioned the curtain into a sort of rudimentary burnoose and secured it by tying the autumnal cravat as a headband around Luther's brow, square dancers do-si-doing up and down his spine, little snowballs a-dangle on his forehead. Rexroat took up the chiffon train and flung it, with a Lawrence of Arabia flourish and an audible sigh of relief, about the lower portion of Luther's visage, then stepped back and declared his creation a worthy rival to the Sheik of Araby.

"Behold, madam!" he exulted. "Out of Egypt have I called my son! Behold Abdul the Assyrian, the Infidel with the Mark of Satan upon His Countenance and the Love of Jay-zis in His Heart!"

20

"Yas, Jay-zis!" echoed the Infidel. "I'm gone, Grannie! Amen goddamn, I am gone!"

"Hesh, mister!" snapped the doting matriarch. "I'll have that first ten cash on the barrelhead," she announced, turning to Rexroat. "I need to git me some good baloney, for I have et all the groundhog I can stand."

Within the hour they were on their way. Rexroat and Luther rode together in the LaSalle's front seat, His Eminence waxing theosophical at the wheel, Luther riding shotgun, grinning behind his veil as if he found the archbishop's every utterance immeasurably enlightening. The backseat was the exclusive domain of Rexroat's other disciple, a decrepit elderly wino roustabout by the name of Bikey, who served as a sort of curate of the Canvas Cathedral.

"And now, my sons," the reverend declaimed after their first few miles on the road, waving his unlit stogie at the windshield as though he were conducting a symphony of himself, "let us take sweet counsel together. Why do the heathen rage, you ask? I'll tell you why, my lads. Because the way of the transgressor is hard! Because the serpent abideth in the garden! Because the king of terrors stalks the earth, while Hell enlarges itself daily! Yea, verily, I have seen all Israel scattered upon the hills, as sheep that have not a shepherd, and doubtless there are those among them that wouldn't pay a nickel to see a pissant eat a bale of hay! But *we* shall shepherd them, Luther my boy! Together, you and I shall drive the wolf from the fold and teach the children of Israel that above all things, the Lord loveth a cheerful giver!"

"Amen, by god!" cried Abdul the Infidel.

"On the dot!" Bikey chimed in from the backseat. "On the dot, Reverent, on the dot!"

"Wherefore," quoth His Reverence, "take unto you the whole armor of God, that you may withstand the evil day! For the worm shall feed sweetly, my sons, on those that rebel against the light! And as for thee, Luther, dear boy, thou shalt become an astonishment, a proverb, and a byword among all nations!"

———

Rexroat proved as good as his word in the matter of faithfully mailing Sallie her weekly stipend—perhaps because, as a man of the cloth, he was also something of a metaphysician and could claim a healthy respect for the Weird Sisterhood, and he understood all too well that anything—absolutely anything—is possible.

Anyhow, he could afford it, for the Assyrian Infidel proved to be a great success among the heathen Pentecostals, and the Canvas Cathedral Worldwide Missionary and Universal Temperance Fund was bringing in the sheaves. When Luther, unveiled, stood at the pulpit and sang, in a cracked but surprisingly sweet and plaintive tenor—a voice, people said, not unlike the peeping, piping tones of the tree frogs on a summer's evening—"Just as I am, I come, I come / O Lamb of God, I come, I come," no Christian heart could have remained unmoved, no Christian purse untapped.

Thus did a certain grinning little green incubus insinuate himself into the bad dreams of more than a few virtuous farmwives.

In due time, the reverend gentleman introduced his acolyte to the pleasures of Four Roses Blended Whiskey, and in the Canvas Cathedral many a midnight toast was lifted to the great Crusade for Universal Temperance.

As a sideline, meanwhile, Rexroat industriously worked the widow-woman dodge at every stop, finding his way several nights a week to the dinner table—and not infrequently to the bed and the bank account—of one or another lonely local matron. Often he returned to the tent with a plate of leftover cold fried chicken and biscuits, a generous donation to the Missionary Fund—and a glow of immense personal satisfaction.

"Hiho, lads!" he'd hail his disciples, hoisting a fresh pint of Four Roses. "Arise from your beds, shake the dew off your lilies, turn up the lamp, break out your tin cups, and let us have ourselves a taste of ignorant oil! For I have caused the widow's heart to sing for joy, and payday comes upon the morrow!"

While Luther and Bikey ate, Rexroat would regale them with tales of his conquest of the evening, never failing to express his gratitude to the Almighty for having placed in his humble servant's way such a cornucopia of blessings.

"Y'know," said Luther one evening, ruminatively gnawing the last drumstick, "*I* shoulda been a preacher. I like fried chicken and dicky-doodle better'n anybody."

"On the dot!" Bikey whooped, his wit by now well lubricated by more than his rightful share of ignorant oil. "And gets lesser of it, too, I reckon . . . with all them noses!"

"Never you mind, Luther, my chuck," soothed the archbishop, as Bikey helped himself to another generous allotment from the pint. "The Lord tempers the wind to the shorn lamb, and sweeter than sweet are the uses of adversity! He who is despised and rejected of men, yea, verily, he who is ugly and venomous like the toad—nothing personal, dear boy—he is a man of sorrows, acquainted of grief . . . yet he wears a precious jewel in his head! Let us find tongues in brooks, and sermons in stones and what have you, and good in . . . Well, let us find good wherever we are so fortunate as to find it!"

"Say again the part about that precious jewel," Luther wheedled.

"In days of yore, my lad, the lowly toad was held to be a sacred beast, possessed of the wisdom of the ages and the sages. And upon its death, its brain was thought to ossify and become, over time, a certain small gemstone—the precious jewel, don't you know, because in the right hands it has, ah, remarkable properties. It's . . . Egad, see here!"

Suddenly Rexroat fell to his knees on the floor of the tent and began pawing through the straw, as though he'd spotted something of great value, perhaps—zounds!—the very object under discussion!

"See here! What cosmogonic confluence of the cosmos is this?"

Rexroat held to the light a small, plum-colored stone—which Luther instantly snatched from the reverend's hand and popped into his mouth, then just as promptly spat it out again, depositing it livid and shimmering in his palm.

"What the billy goddamn hell?" he demanded.

"Gadzooks, lad, it's . . . a toadstone!"

Luther eyed it suspiciously. "Be damn," he said, "I thought it was a chicken liver."

"This, my chub, is the tenth migration of the ossified malignum! Formed by the miracle of petrifaction upon the

perfect corpus of the sacred toad! Keep this sanctified artifact upon your person at all times"—he took Luther's other
hand and closed it over the one that held the stone—"and
look to it in times of trouble, for there might be no end of
luck in it, no end of luck and power and magic!"

"Well then," Luther demanded, "if it's such a booger,
how come you don't keep it yourself?"

"Because, my boy, I don't believe in toadstones, and so it
would be of no use to me. *I* believe, as you have perhaps observed, in the Main Chance, and although there are those
who can tailor their beliefs to suit the demands of the moment, I am not, alas, amongst that happy number. But if I
were you, dear boy, circumstanced as you are in the matter of,
ah, affinities and what-have-you, I should declare my faith in
toadstones, indeed I should."

"Be damn." Luther peeked between his fingers cau-
tiously, as though he half expected the captive stone to slither
free and go bounding off for the nearest toadstool.

"Watch out now!" Bikey hooted. "Them rocks is hard
to catch!"

"Be not deterred by Philistines and skeptics, dear boy!
There are millions of rocks, millions and billions, but precious few are toadstones! Who can say what powers reside
within it? You and I are but poor students of the great mystery of life, and the first lesson we must learn is to take nothing for granted! Nothing!"

"On the dot!" howled Bikey, in a perfect transport of
Dutch courage. "Specially not when some lyin' ol' shit-
pitcher like Rexroat tells it to you!"

Luther and Rexroat exchanged a look that would have

sobered Bikey on the spot if he hadn't been too drunk to appreciate it. Then Luther pocketed the stone, hooked back his last drop of Four Roses, and took himself off to bed, to dream, we must assume, of widow women and fried chicken.

When Bikey awoke the next morning, he found himself under a blazing sun in the middle of a vacant lot, with no Canvas Cathedral sheltering him and no LaSalle, no trailer, no Rexroat, no Luther, no payday, and most lamentable of all—considering his condition—not a dram of ignorant oil. Yet Bikey was withal more fortunate than he knew—for Luther had stoutly urged the reverend to run over him a time or two on their way out.

————

Back at her wet-mop, Juanita labors grimly, struggling to prepare herself for what she knows she has to do.

Warren Harding Skidmore is the daddy of this baby that's inside her, and sometimes Juanita halfway wishes she could just go ahead and have it, just for spite—because, being his, it will have red hair, and everybody will know he was the one that did it.

But there's another thing: in her heart, Juanita fears that if she has this baby, she will love it more than she can stand—and that if she doesn't have it, she will hate herself forever—and all because Warren Harding is its daddy.

Warren Harding Skidmore is the only child of a briefly successful Burdock County insurance salesman who died young and left behind a tidy little property, a hopelessly chuckleheaded widow, and an infant heir who proved constitutionally disposed to take full advantage of both circumstances. The widow Skidmore, in her grief, lugubriously pampered and petted and indulged the boy to a high gloss, thereby assuring herself of a son who would grow up devious, dissolute, thieving, and mean. At ten he was a tormentor of cats and turpentiner of dogs, at twelve a lifter of little girls' skirts; by fifteen he was stealing his despairing mother blind; by seventeen he'd wrecked three cars, two of them while trying to run down small animals.

Recently, to reward the likely lad for having finally cheated and bullied his way through high school, his feckless parent had bought him the Pinhook Texaco station from the estate of the lately dispatched Lugnut Bludgins—and then promptly dithered and fretted herself into a fit of apoplexy and an early grave when she found out he used the station mostly as a place to pitch pennies and play gin rummy and lay up drunk with the local sporting set.

One afternoon back in the early autumn, Juanita's Uncle Dutch had taken Luther Jukes out and handcuffed him to a lawn mower and put him to mowing the courthouse yard, and while he was mowing (Juanita saw the whole thing from the courthouse porch, where she was washing the windows of the sheriff's office), Warren Harding drove around and around the block hollering smart remarks—"Hey! You cut grass like a man with two noses!"—and one time, he leaned out the car window and threw an apple core and hit the prisoner on the leg

Juanita is scared spitless of the two-nosed man, but she ain't the kind that likes to see anybody get tormented.

But the meanest trick of all—Juanita reflects, often and bitterly—was the one Warren Harding did on Juanita her own self. Because if you must know, she really, truly loved him, see—that red, red hair, y'know, and . . . oh! them freckles!—and that's why he was the first one she had ever, you know, *went* with, if you can call it going with somebody which never took her anywheres except the graveyard, to park and get in the backseat. Many a time he'd have her back at the jail inside of thirty minutes. But a person needs something nice in their life even if it don't last but thirty minutes, so she put up with it.

Then, one night a couple of months ago—the very night that Juanita was planning to tell Warren Harding that she had missed her curse again this month, and what did he aim to do about it?—Warren Harding got out of the car after he was done, and went around and opened up the trunk, and . . . and out come that sneakin' Sharky Vance! So then Warren Harding went over and set down on a tombstone and commenced to clean his fingernails like he thought he was the King of Sheba, while Sharky just politely hopped in the backseat with Juanita!

At first, Juanita thought she would just kick Sharky in his textacles again, like she had in eighth grade, and then get out and walk home. But she seen in her heart that Warren Harding didn't give a poot what happened to her one way or the other, and if Sharky Vance hopped around on her till next Tuesday she couldn't get no more pragnent than she already was, and anyhow she felt so low-down and lonesome that she was halfway glad for the company.

So one thing led to another thing, and directly here she is two months later, still p.g. and not but one person in the world which can tell her where to turn, and that's a person with . . . two noses.

Disencumbered of Bikey, Abdul the Infidel had become, under Rexroat's tutelage, ever more indispensable to the archbishop's salvational exertions. The reverend gentleman coached him in how to talk in tongues—no problem for an Assyrian—and how to fling himself to the ground twitching and frothing in a paroxysm of Christian zeal, and how to rifle the ladies' purses while their owners were similarly enthralled. After every service, the two pious entrepreneurs moved among the congregation hawking—at a dollar-fifty per, marked down from five ninety-eight—autographed copies of a pamphlet entitled *Prayers for My Good Health*, by the Reverend P. Cosmo Rexroat, Doctor of Natural Theosophy, Chiropractic Science, and Colonic Irrigation—who had already assiduously instructed Luther in the numerous arcane arts of shortchanging the clientele. The money changers had, at long last, turned the tables on the Christians.

His Eminence even revealed, in an attack of candor brought on one evening by a sacramental beaker of Four Roses, that the oversized volume that was always open before him on the pulpit was not exactly the Holy Bible so much as it was, in point of fact, *Bartlett's Familiar Quotations*.

Eventually, after many seasons on the road, they happened to cross trails with a carnival that employed a lady of the reverend's acquaintance, the former star attraction of a skin joint called Uncle Billy Peeper's Wild West Revue, where she'd performed as Nyoka, Queen of the Apaches. A few years back, when Rexroat was running a three-card monte flat just down the midway, they'd managed a little tumble in the hay while Uncle Billy's peepers were turned elsewhere. These days—Uncle Billy having lately overtaxed his central nervous system and been gathered unto his fathers—she was plain Wanda Pearl Ratliff once again, selling tickets for the Tilt-A-Whirl, waiting, like Mr. Micawber, for something to turn up.

"And not no goddamn hide show neither, hon," she told her confidential friend Gertrude, who worked the cotton candy stand. "It ain't polite, showin' your spizzerinctum to a bunch of strangers at my age."

When something did turn up, in the persons of Rexroat and his remarkable disciple, the two former lovers elected to throw in together and resume their raptures. Rexroat, with Luther at his side, turned immediately to his *Bartlett's*, this time falling amongst the poets. After a few hours of deep study, they took the cross off the top of the trailer and joined the carnival, setting up shop as Colonel Rexroat and His Amazing Two-Nosed Child Prodigy, Little Luther the Appalachian Frog Boy. Never mind that the Child Prodigy was old enough to vote or that his genius was represented solely by his ability to recite, at a snap of the newly commissioned colonel's fingers, a few lines from "Invictus," or "Thanatopsis," or "The Boy Stood on the Burning Deck."

"This, m'dear," the colonel predicted to Wanda Pearl in an aside on opening night, "will be a strong joint. The general public, you see, loves a freak with book sense best of all. It confirms their darkest suspicions about intelligence and reassures them that when all is said and done, ignorance is still a virtue."

As usual, when it came to human nature, Colonel Rexroat had it dead on the money: it *was* a strong joint.

Whether they came to admire Luther's noses or his intellect—or maybe just because it only cost fifteen cents to enjoy what the colonel, in his grind, liked to call "the whole shit-a-ree, dear hearts!"—the Two-Nosed Child Prodigy drew good crowds.

". . . She drove her daughter, great with child, from her door into the storm!" went the Rexroatian rendition of Luther's history, while Luther stood by, masked to the eyes by a red bandanna. "Yea, and with the storm raging all around her, friends, this unnatural mother cried, 'And may your firstborn be a brother to the toad!' "

However (Rexroat would explain), because the unborn child was inadvertently her own grandson, the ethics of the Sisterhood had required the crone to accompany her curse with a special endowment of some kind, a gift, a blessing. After thinking it through, she cunningly decided to grant him overarching intelligence, that he might always know he was . . . a frog.

"A cruel hoax, my friends! Better she had made the lad an imbecile! But his loss is Western civilization's gain, dear hearts, and now you can see the entire phenomenon for a mere fifteen cents, the whole in-ta lec̄tual shit-a-ree for three greasy little nickels . . ."

(In due time, while he languished in that Missouri prison under the tutelage of the learned safecracker, Luther, fingering his toadstone, would ruminate long and deeply upon Rexroat's fanciful account of how a likely lad such as himself came to be that which he indisputably was—a frog boy, no getting 'round it—and would eventually conclude that his own doting old grannie was indeed the bane of his infelicitous existence. Accordingly, those of us who know our

Luther's character may safely assume that until he was un-avoidably detained in Pinhook by the fateful encounter with Lugnut Bludgins, he was on his way to pay a social call at the old log house on Morgadore, and that Bad-Cess Sallie would not have been made comfortable by the prodigal's return.)

After the colonel had inveigled an audience into the tent, he'd break out his old three-card monte setup and, while they waited for the Prodigy to display his extraordinary proper-ties, would endeavor—successfully, as a rule—to disengage a few among them from their pocket money.

"Lord, hon, he's slick as snot on a goddamn doorknob!" said Wanda Pearl admiringly to Gertrude. "Last night he jiggered a mark outta seventeen dollars quick as a pick-pocket, and two minutes later he's got the two-nose sayin' a poem about Down by the Shores of Glitchy-Gloomy, and the mark is cryin' like a goddamn orphan!"

Alas, their success was short-lived. For at the Arbuckle County Fair in Eggermont, Missouri, that injudicious dep-uty sheriff saw fit to inquire how many flies Luther had et so far that day . . . and a few hours later, Luther waylaid him down by the stables and beat him senseless with a singletree. Southeast Missouri being intolerant of ill-natured Frog Boys from out of state, they charged him with the attempted mur-der of a lawman and set about to throw away the key.

While Luther awaited trial, Rexroat paid him a farewell visit at the Arbuckle County slam. He and Wanda Pearl, the colonel said, had bought themselves a two-headed chicken and were looking around for a few pickled punks and maybe a half-and-half. So they'd be moving on.

"We'll miss you, my lad," he said, taking his leave, "in-

deed we will. You could have been the strongest blow-off going. It's an incalculable loss to Western civilization. But"—
Colonel Rexroat sighed, shrugged extravagantly, and turned
to go—"but, as the philosopher says, that's show business."

Juanita has mopped her way almost to his cell door, and
nobody in the whole jail but him and her, and she knows that
if she's ever going to say something to him, now's the time.
But she can't hardly just waltsch right up to him and say,
Welp, Mr. Two-Nose, how much would that old woman
charge me to get rid of this here baby? What she needs is
something nice and friendly to kind of break the ice a little,
something along the line of Welp, Mr. Two-Nose, it's a nice
day out, ain't it? But then she thinks, What's it to him, *he*
ain't out.

So when she stops in front of his cell to wring out her
mop, she still don't have the least ideal what she's going to say.
Nonetheless, steeling herself to look at him without flinching, she straightens up over the mop bucket and takes a deep
breath and opens her mouth and—

"Thirty-five dollars."

"Hunh?"

"Thirty-five dollars, cash on the barrelhead. Them's
Grannie's rates."

The voice issues from the gloomy recesses of the cell—
wherein, to her relief, Juanita sees that our Luther is wearing his bandanna and so looks less like a monster, if more
like a burglar. But the price he's named is so stupendous
(the county pays Juanita nine dollars a week, Aunt Jimmie
charges her six for room and board, and right now she's got

two dollars and forty cents to her name) that she forgets to wonder how he's answered a question she hadn't even asked yet.

"It ain't me!" she blurts. "I was just askin' for, uh, . . . Harletta Porch. This friend of mine. Is who it was."

"Listen," he says, in a voice muffled and made ominous by the bandanna, "people pays good money to look at me, but it don't cross their mind that I'm a-looking back at them. I can see through you like a drink of water."

Juanita lowers her eyes, as though she stands before a stern, all-knowing judge, pleading guilty. She knows, deep inside herself, that her life has reached a turning point.

"It was that redheaded jack, I reckon. Oh, I seen you sneakin' out at night, oh, yes! I seen him pick you up out yonder in the jail yard! I knowed what you all was up to, you bet, oh, yes!"

Luther's eloquence suggests that that little matter of the apple core has not quite been forgotten.

"Anyhow," he continues, less vehemently, "you don't want to let Grannie get her hooks in you, she's a bad egg. She ain't the one you need."

"Who, then?" Juanita pleads.

"Why, me, that's who. Me, myself, and I. Now I can't knock that baby for you, that's Grannie's line of work. But lookahere"—he steps to the bars and lowers his voice to a conspiratorial whisper—"there's more than one way to skin a cat. What if I could show you how to make that Skidmore do right by you?"

Juanita, in her desperation, has even prayed to God to help her out, but it looks to her like the Devil is the one that answered.

"You can make him—?"

"I can make him *marry* you!"

"How?"

"All right," he whispers, "you know them shoe boxes in the office?"

Juanita does; he means the ones on the shelf behind Uncle Dutch's desk where the jailer keeps the odds and ends he takes out of prisoners' pockets when they go to jail.

"Well, one of them boxes," Luther goes on, "has got my name on it, and in that box is a little purple rock, about so big. You sneak in there this afternoon while he's out 'lectioneering, and you get me that little rock and bring it to me around about midnight, when they're all asleep, and I'll show you a secret trick that works like . . . a charm."

"Uh-huh," says Juanita. "And what's this trick gonna cost me?"

"Not a penny. But when you come"—he points out of the gloom to the key ring at her waist—"you bring them keys."

"Oh, Lord," Juanita gasps. "You ain't aiming to run off? Uncle Dutch'll break my neck!"

"Run off? Hell no," he tells her, with a dry little laugh. "I ain't coming out, you're coming in."

———

Now here's Juanita sitting in the dark in her little room, waiting for midnight. She sits near the window, hands in her lap; her right hand, palm up, cradles the toadstone. A harvest moon hangs over Needmore, and a vagrant moonbeam has singled out the Sanctified Artifact so that it seems almost to glow with an inner light as Juanita gazes abstractedly down upon it, trying to figure out what in the h-e-double-l she ought to do.

Yes, she had stole the rock, like he told her to, but she could put that back any old time, Uncle Dutch'd never know the difference. And she never has been one to take much stock in spells and curses and rabbit feet and all. She ain't a bit religious.

On the other hand, she remembers the time her little brother Herschel got the mumps, and Grandma Souseley tied a blue silk ribbon around his waist to keep them from dropping on him, and they never did drop. So who knows, you can't tell, maybe there's something to it after all.

Although Juanita's heart is as capacious as the bosom in which it is lodged, she realizes she's not no Miss Gantley in the brains department. Still, she can see just exactly what will happen if she lets Uncle Dutch and Aunt Jimmie send her back to the homeplace to have the baby. There wouldn't be no peace for her in this life, that's for sure. Old spiteful Aunt Augusta wouldn't let her out of her sight; the only social life she'd have for the rest of her days would be cleaning up after all them Souseleys. Which when you think about it ain't that different from her social life right now, except the Souseleys wouldn't be locked up in the drunk tank, they'd be running around loose. And her sweet little redheaded baby, even though it'd be a Sparks by name and half Skidmore by blood, would be bound to get some Souseley on it while it was growing up.

All this Juanita sees as plain as day, almost as if it has already happened. Yet if she did but know it, at this very moment she holds, literally in the palm of her hand, an altogether different future. For the toadstone encompasses all knowledge, and if it could speak—or rather, if she knew how to listen to it—it would tell her things she's never dreamed of.

But Luther Jukes hears the toadstone's voice, clear as a nightingale's; it sings to him of luck and power and magic, exactly as told by the prophet Rexroat. If Juanita brings the plenipotent relic to him in his cell, she'll discover that other life which, we devoutly hope, awaits her. . . .

Tomorrow morning, just as the sun is coming up, she will awaken from a sleep so deep and so untroubled it could almost have been a kind of trance. She'll be in Warren Harding Skidmore's car; he is at the wheel, and she's been sleeping with her head pillowed on his thigh. She knows whose car it is and whose thigh it is, because the first thing she sees when she opens her eyes is this raw-knuckled, freckled hand on the suicide knob, with the 1941 Burdock County High School class ring on the ring finger, a hand she knows almost as well as the hand knows her.

There's a voice somewhere inside her head, saying—no, not a voice, exactly, just the words theirselves, kind of scratchy and screechy, like a memory of something Miss Gantley could've wrote, one time long ago, on the black-board:

> The iron tongue of midnight hath told twelve;
> Lovers, to bed; 'tis almost fairy time.

Juanita has no idea where she is or where they're going, yet a warm, delicious feeling of contentment and perfect trust steals over her. Gratefully, she closes her eyes again and drifts back into sleep, and as she does she will hear, oh, my, the most amazing thing, Warren Harding Skidmore, somewhere far above her, murmuring, ever so softly, "Maud Muller on a summer's day, raked the meadow sweet with hay . . ."

Back in the jailer's house in Needmore, Aunt Jimmie, as she sleepily goes about assembling breakfast, will chance upon a note on her kitchen table. "Me and Waren Harding S.," it reads, "has run off 2 get married." The note is signed, "You're neace, Juanita Sparks."

And even as Aunt Jimmie stands there shaking her head in disbelief—"The child don't know poop from apple butter!"—the morning quiet will be rent by a bloodcurdling shriek of anguish from the jail, of which, as we know, Luther Jukes is currently the sole inhabitant.

The prisoner has awakened under a strange delusion: he believes—or at any rate he hysterically professes to believe—that as recently as last night he had been a free man and that the free man he had been was, of all people, Warren Harding Skidmore. Last night, around about midnight, after dropping off his running mates Sharky and Dime, he—Warren Harding Skidmore—under the influence of a few (quite a few) beers, had pulled into the jail yard—hoping, perhaps, that Juanita's dreams would inspire her to go out walking in her sleep, looking for him—and had gone to sleep himself instead. . . .

He awakes in jail. Bringing his hand to his aching head—whoever made off with the corporeal Warren Harding S. having neglected to take along his hangover—he discovers that overnight he has somehow acquired—*Aieeee!*—a second nose!

This likely story will be greeted, predictably, by a chorus of derision and ridicule. The vast preponderance of opinion will hold that of course the murderer, in his infernal cunning, hopes to cheat the hangman by pleading insanity; a much smaller number choose to believe that he has in fact lost his mind, because only a genuine lunatic could concoct such a story in the first place.

Tomorrow evening, the return of the newlyweds—for such they are, absolutely—will affirm that Warren Harding Skidmore's outer man is thoroughly intact and appears to be none the worse for the purported transmigration of his soul.

When the prisoner, confronted with this new evidence, persists in banging his head against the bars and tearing his hair and, variously, shrieking and screaming and howling and moaning words to the effect that *he* is Warren Harding Skidmore—even though the fact that he's Luther Jukes is (in the amused opinion of Warren Harding, who almost overnight seems to have metamorphosed from rather a dullard into what passes locally for something of a wag) "as plain as the noses on his face"—a few neighborhood ancients will begin reminding each other that the rottenest apple falls nearest the tree, and Lord knows what all a grandchild of Bad-Cess Sallie Jukes might do.

But when the howling and shrieking and head banging—"Sounds like he's in there playin' dodgeball with a brick!" quipped Warren Harding, on the occasion of his first supper with his new in-laws, the Louderbacks—and moaning and screaming and so on and so forth continue unabated throughout the next few weeks before the trial, the weight of public sentiment will have shifted, gradually but inexorably, toward the conclusion that the unhappy prisoner is indeed quite mad.

Then too, as the trial date approaches, those who had known Lugnut Bludgins in life will perhaps acknowledge to themselves that they can't honestly say they miss him much; their eulogies of him rarely extend beyond Luther Jukes's own encomium to the effect that Lugnut was, in fact, too goddamn dumb to live. In any event, by court day there will have developed in the public mind a certain sympathy for the afflicted wretch who's been setting up such a hee-cack in the county jail.

At his trial, Luther Jukes—he who is called Luther Jukes—has to be dragged into the courtroom in a straitjacket; and as the sheriff's deputies seat him in the dock, an evil-looking old crone amongst the spectators—Bad-Cess Sallie, of course, showing remarkable agility for her years—will leap to her feet and point a long, yellow-nailed finger at the defendant, screeching again and again, "It ain't him! It ain't him! You bloomin' idjits, it ain't him!"

She will have to be escorted from the courtroom, while the prisoner in the dock, quiescent for once, looks on uncomprehendingly.

After that brief outburst, justice will move swiftly, and before the day is done Luther Jukes—he who is called Luther Jukes—will be declared innocent by reason of insanity and committed to spend the rest of his days in a padded cell in the Commonwealth's most dismal madhouse—quite possibly the same institution to which, many years before, the Bludgins committee had sought to consign an earlier manifestation of our amiable friend—where perhaps he may find time to mourn all the small animals he's run over.

As the deputies lead the wretched prisoner away, there will rise above the general hubbub in the spectators gallery a male voice cheerily calling out, "And forever, O my brother, hail and farewell!" Several nearby spectators later agree that the voice was that of Warren Harding Skidmore—of he, that is, who calls himself Warren Harding Skidmore. Certainly, however, not one among them suspects that the former dullard's words were borrowed from Catullus.

That very night, the peaceful dreams of downtown Pinhook will be broken by the clang of the village fire bell—too late, alas, for the old log house on Morgadore will have burned to the ground, with Bad-Cess Sallie in it, by the time the fire engine turns down her lane. Officially, the fire can only be attributed to a defective coal oil heater, but there will always be those in Burdock County who believe—who profess to believe—that the flash point was old Sallie herself in her featherbed and that the cause was spontaneous combustion.

The ruins smoldered for days, they say, and the stench of sulphur fouled the air for miles around.

The new Mr. and Mrs. Skidmore, meanwhile, will have gone to housekeeping like any other young couple, and Warren Harding—the new Warren Harding—will have utterly thrown over his old wicked ways and bad companions, as every young breadwinner must, and buckled himself into the traces and gone to work. By the time the excitement of the Jukes trial has begun fading into history, Skidmore Texaco, fresh as paint and elbow grease can make it, is the tidiest, most forward-looking business establishment in downtown

Pinhook, and Harletta Porch is up to her plucked eyebrows in plans for her friend Juanita's baby shower.

Before the year is out, America will find itself yet again in the toils of a great war; the following spring, Warren Harding's number in the military draft will come up on the same day that Juanita presents him with a ruddy, squalling, red-headed draft deferment. And every eleven months for the duration of the war, dependable as the seasons, she will repeat the ceremony, so that by the war's end there will be four spanking new Skidmores, with a fifth on the way, and Warren Harding won't have been required to dodge a single bullet.

Skidmore Texaco will by then have become Skidmore Used Cars, soon to be Skidmore Used Cars and Ford-Ferguson Tractors, then Skidmore Ford ("Out of the High-Rent District!"), then Skidmore Ford-Mercury-Lincoln (by now W. H.—as he calls himself—is much in demand at the annual Lions Club Fourth of July picnic for his famously stirring recitation of Longfeller's immortal "Paul Revere's Ride" and is widely regarded as Burdock County's leading patriot and intellect), and so on down through the years until the dealership acquires so many titles, both domestic and foreign ("Skidmore Ford-Mercury-Lincoln-Porsche-Volvo-Toyota-Hyundai-Peugeot-Subaru") and occupies so much territory that at last it positively swallows whole the village of Pinhook and becomes a sort of city-state in its own right, populated largely by automobiles . . .

. . . by which time those five little Skidmores will have taken over the several ethnic neighborhoods of the dealership, each to his or her own little principality, and Warren Harding and Juanita are safely ensconced in a condo—"condominimum," W. H. calls it, with a flash of his old wit—in West Fungo Beach Golfing Community in West Fungo Beach, Florida, where Juanita whiles away her golden years playing canasta with some nice Jewish ladies while W. H. goes a-golfing, his lucky toadstone keeping company with the loose change in his pocket.

———

But none of this has happened yet, and for all we know it will never happen—for Juanita, remember, is at this moment still sitting at the window in her lonely little room, glumly pensive, pondering the decision that will seal her fate.

In her palm, the toadstone seems almost to pulse with light, like a tiny, luminous heart, beating hard, as though it were trying desperately to tell her something.

And now the courthouse clock tolls thrice. It must be midnight.

The
CONGRESS
of
WONDERS

1.

"This way, this way, this way, this way, it's sensational, it's terrific, it's educational, it's scientific! Marvels and monstrosities, freaks of nature and facts of life, miracles of modern medical science, throwbacks to the Dark Ages of his-toh-ree! See the immortal Lord's Prayer engraved by the finest Hebrew scribes of ancient Abyssinia upon the head of a priceless sterling silver pin! See Little Big, the World's Smallest Midget Donkey! See the lovely and talented Bearded Contessa, toast of seven continents! See the Chicken Boy, Miracle Baby of Bunchburg, in the great state of Tenn-oh-see! See it all, my friends, right here at the Burdock County Fair, amaze yourself and amuse yourself at the incredible Congress of Wonders, brought to you at exorbitant expense by yours truly, Professor Philander Cosmo Rexroat, B.S., M.S., and *Pee*"—Professor Rexroat lowers his megaphone, ceremoniously doffs his pith helmet to the milling midway, mops his damp, florid brow with his shirtsleeve, and covers his thinning silver senatorial locks again—"Aitch Dee, direct from the Instituto del Experimento Scientifico of Nuevo Laredo, Mexico, internationally acclaimed explorer, globe-trotter, author, archaeologist, zoologist, ichthyologist, herpetologist, lepidopterist, philatelist, cosmologist, natural theosophist, minister of the Gospel, and licensed practitioner of colonic irrigation! This way, this way, this way! See the lovely and talented Patagonian Mermaid, whose charms have sent many a dee-lirious seaman to the briny deep! See the Two-Headed Pig, the Hairless Jackanape, the Five-Legged Calf, the Three-Eyed Tasmanian Boa Constrictor, the Fur-Bearing Web-Footed Hornswoggle, see curiosities previously exhibited only before the crowned heads of Europe! . . ."

The professor's spiel rumbles on, an oily fount of hogwash. Professor Rexroat, general all-around Man of Science, Man of Letters, and Man of God, is withal a smallish gent, and his improbably large, dirgelike baritone, issuing from beneath his Frank Buck pith helmet like the sepulchral croak of a bullfrog under a toadstool, strikes a lugubrious note against the tinkling gaiety of the midway. Yet it casts no pall—for this is 1944, the summer of Normandy, the summer of the taking of Guam and Tinian and Saipan, the very week of the liberation of Paris, and in America we are at last beginning to allow ourselves to hope again, and to celebrate such happiness as the war has left to us. So, even as the bright lights of the midway dispel the gathering dusk and the evening chases the sullen heat of the dog-day afternoon, so too does the spirit of rejoicing dissipate the professor's gloomy monotone.

From the painted canvas backdrop behind him, the misbegotten prodigies whose little idiosyncracies the professor is heralding gaze down in lurid color, all apparently very much alive and enjoying vigorous health, notwithstanding the unhappy fact that inside the Congress of Wonders tent, the vast majority of its star attractions are basking in glass vessels of formaldehyde. Nor, indeed, does the professor feel it necessary to notify the public that more than a few among his little troupe of pickled artistes owe their interesting anatomies to the resourcefulness of a certain alcoholic taxidermist in Idabelle, Alabama—who fashioned, for instance, both the Chicken Boy and the Patagonian Mermaid in a single afternoon by dismantling a deceased rhesus monkey, a Rhode Island Red rooster, and a large Perdido River mud cat and then reassembling their several parts according to his recollection of some rather unsettling dreams he'd been having lately. ("Yass, Doc Woosley had a way with leftovers," the professor has often remarked to JoJo, his hermaphrodite, of his old drinking buddy. "The, ah, remains of the rooster furnished the two of us an excellent coq au vin that evening, so only the fish head went to waste.") But in his spiel, Professor Rexroat keeps these little particulars close to his gravy-spangled vest and rumbles on.

"See the death-defying Signorina Electra Spumoni, my dear friends, see this lovely and talented little lady, born to the court of the kings and queens of the Holy Roman Empire, see her cruelly strapped into a genuine authentic certified simulated regulation electric chair, an exact similar replica of the infernal engine in which the lowest elements of modern society meet their untimely end, see her receive into her fair, unblemished, highly refined young person *fif-ty thou-sand deadly volts* of pure electric power! Enough electricity, friends, to run a trolley car nonstop from New York to Los Angeleeze, in the state of Cal-oh-fornia! And back again!"

2.

Near the professor's podium, at a wobbly card table parked before the entryway to the tent, sits a hulking, scowling woman in a long, none-too-clean dressing gown and dusty carpet slippers, smoking furiously, her large head studded like a hand grenade with fierce henna-tinted pin curls. This rara avis is Professor Rexroat's business manager, consort, soul mate, and ingenue, the lovely and talented Signorina Electra Spumoni herself, née Wanda Pearl Ratliff of Ardmore, Oklahoma. On the table before the Signorina are a cash box and a roll of tickets, and directly above her spiky noggin hangs what purports to be her own portrait—a stunning depiction of a bathing beauty wearing a coronet and brandishing, Zeus-like, two fistfuls of lightning bolts, a figure that might have been the result had old Doc Woosley conjoined Betty Grable's gams, Dorothy Lamour's torso, and Shirley Temple's countenance. That the professor will shortly be requiring his clientele to accept this vision as a likeness of the actual Signorina Ratliff in the ample flesh is a testimony to his boundless faith in the credulity of his fellowman.

Almost at Wanda Pearl's shoulder, just outside the rope that separates her table from the midway throngs, stands a boy, a towhead of some twelve or thirteen years, eating a candy apple and gazing raptly up at the masterpiece above him. On the back of his head is perched a white sailor's hat, deeply soiled by much affectionate fondling with grubby fingers.

"Hey, lady," says the boy to the all-too-real Electra at his elbow, never lowering his eyes from the bogus one on the canvas banner, "where's that there 'lectric girl *at*?"

"Inside," says Wanda Pearl, without a flicker of hesitation. "You got a quarter, admiral, you can come in and look at her till yer ship comes in."

"Ain't she pretty, now," he murmurs.

"Pretty as pie," Wanda Pearl assures him. "Girl about your age, too, mm-hmm."

"This way, this way, this way!" drones the professor, deep-mouthed as the grave. "See it all right here at Professor Rexroat's Congress of Wonders! See Joseph/Josephine, the Human Enigma! One half a pu-u-u-ulchritoodinous, vo-o-o-looptuous female in the full bloom of her womanhood, one half a vee-rile male with all his manly faculties intact!" (The extraordinary personage so described is, according to the representation of it on the banner, divided vertically, its right side a mustachioed circus strongman in a leopard-skin undershirt, its left a curvaceous cutie in a tutu.) "The entire Mystery of Life wrapped up in one lovely and talented young body! So shocking that each and every ticket includes, absolutely free of charge, a one-thousand-dollar life insurance policy! Ladies cordially invited!"

"I haven't got no money," the boy owns ruefully. He looks off into the midway crowd, searching, and adds, "My brother and them's got some, though. They got a-plenty."

"Is that him?" Wanda Pearl inquires, peering off in the same direction. "The sailor boy?" The sailor she's got her eye on is across the midway at the baseball pitch, throwing at the flip-overs of Hitler and Tōjō and Mussolini. Another young man, in civvies, and two girls stand by, cheering him on. "I tell you what," she proposes. "You get them four to come in here, I'll let you in free. Won't cost you a penny."

The boy is doubtful. "I dunno," he says, "him and Skinner just took up with them girls a minute ago. They was aiming to take 'em on the Tunnel o' Love, I think. I dunno if they'll . . ."

"Aaaah, sure they will. Tell 'em about the morphadyke. Tell 'em it's a thing they ort to see."

"Well . . ." Then he decides, and suddenly he's off like a shot, already calling, "Hey, Sonny, hey!" A second later Wanda Pearl sees him through the crowd, tugging at the sailor's sleeve and pointing in her direction. Ain't that cute now, she chuckles. She always did have a soft spot for little old boys like that, ever since she was a girl back home in Ardmore.

The professor's pitch is beginning to reel 'em in. Approaching Wanda Pearl's table now is a tall, shambling rube with a look of irremediable puzzlement about the eyes. He is accompanied by two women, one work-worn and old-looking, the other—his daughter, to judge by her own long chin and idiot eyes—no more than fourteen or fifteen, both enormously pregnant, the latter doubtless bearing a likely candidate for one of the professor's jugs of formaldehyde. Christ on a crutch, Wanda Pearl reflects, sighing, while the rube digs three quarters from his old leather snap purse. What a world, what a goddamn world. It's more freaks outside the show as inside, nowadays.

3.

The two young men over at the baseball pitch are Gunner's Mate Third Class Wilbur D. "Sonny" Capto Jr., USN, and his old pal Skinner Worthington, 4-F. Sonny Capto, a perfect picture of a lad, with crinkly, golden curls and eyes as blue as cornflowers and a head as empty as all outdoors, is presently enjoying the sixteenth day of his last twenty-one-day shore leave; some eighteen hours from now, he will board a train in Cincinnati, and four days later—though of course this is a military secret, so Sonny doesn't know it yet—he'll pass beneath the Golden Gate aboard the MS *Avenger*, a minesweeper bound for the South Pacific. His companion, Skinner Worthington, a gangly youth with an incipient potbelly and a million-dollar heart murmur, can claim no such exciting prospects; tomorrow morning—and every workday morning for the ensuing forty years—he will be at his post in Worthington & Son's Ladies' Footwear Emporium in Needmore, across the street from the Burdock County courthouse.

Sonny and Skinner have been running mates since Burdock County High School, a partnership to which Skinner has traditionally contributed the wheels and finances while Sonny has put up the good looks. Tonight, having already secured them the attentions of a tolerably pretty girl for Sonny and a tolerably homely one for Skinner, their collaboration seems to be functioning about as successfully as it used to. And the girls—a brace of consummately trashy gum-popping blondes named, by odd coincidence, Rosemary and Rosemary—appear ready, willing, and indefatigably able to send Sonny off to war and Skinner back to his daddy's shoe store in a state of blissful enervation.

Regrettably, there is a rather substantial fly in the two young gallants' ointment tonight, in the innocent person of Wade Capto, Sonny's little brother, whom Sonny has brought along over Skinner's grumblings and who is even at this very moment plucking at the sleeve of Sonny's middy blouse, breathlessly imploring him to consider including the Congress of Wonders in the evening's entertainment.

"They got a two-headed pig, and a five-legged calf, and . . ."

"Hot damn, Sunset," Skinner chortles, nudging Sonny with an elbow, "sounds like your old man's farm!" Skinner's own idea of the evening's entertainment, consistent with his standard wooing procedure, is to get one of these Rosemarys into a dark place somewhere and run his hand up her leg and see what happens. He ain't studying no two-headed pig.

". . . and a chicken boy," Wade goes on, undaunted, "and a three-eyed boar conscriptor, and . . ."

"Is this yore baby bruvver, Sonny?" whoops Big Rosie, a strapping Aphrodite with the voice of a bugling coonhound. "Ain't he a doll!"

"Lookit his li'l sailor cap!" shrieks the dumpy Little Rosie, with less volume but equal stridor. "He is such a doll!"

"Kid thinks I hung the moon," Sonny modestly confides, tossing a baseball from hand to hand. "He hasn't hardly took off that swabbie hat since I give it to him. Have you now, shipmate?"

Wade ignores them all as best he can and presses on. "And they got the Lord's Prayer on a pinhead, and a . . . a marthadyke, and . . ."

"Nah," Sonny is declining, "see, shipmate, me and Skin, we . . ."

"Hold it, kiddo," Skinner breaks in. "They got a morphadyke, you say?" Wade has hooked himself a live one.

"Oooo, icksy!" the two Rosemarys scream, as in a single voice. "A old morphadyke! Let's go see it, you all!"

"It's a thing you *ort* to see!" Wade urges, remembering the ticket lady's exhortation. "And they got one of these fish-girls that don't wear no clothes on her . . ."—he gulps, and blushes as red as his candy apple, and lowers his voice almost to a whisper, but he gets it said—"on her . . . boozems, and . . ."

Amid peals of girlish laughter, Skinner turns to Sonny and says, with a wink and a smirk, "Whaddya say, Cap'n Capto? I reckon we could take these gals to see the morphadyke, don't you?"

Sonny grins his accord, takes off his swabbie hat and claps it, starched and bleached white as a new tooth, atop Big Rosemary's towering, mustard-colored upsweep. Then he wheels and lets fly with the baseball, and pops old Tōjō right between the eyes, flipping him over to show his naked, bristly yellow hiney. The attendant hands Sonny a pea-green monkey on a stick, which Sonny straightway passes on to the clangorously ecstatic Big Rosie. If she hadn't been there, it would've been Wade's monkey, sure. From beneath his own soiled cap, Wade glares at Big Rosemary as though he can't believe they're in the same navy.

"See it all, see it here, see it now!" they hear the professor calling from across the midway. "See it all at the amazing Congress of Wonders! It's scientific, it's sensational, it's . . ."

"C'mon, shipmates," Sonny says, throwing an arm around Big Rosemary's shoulders. "Anchors aweigh. Let's go reconnoiter that there morphadyke."

4.

"See the amazing Bodiless Head! A human head actually *severed from its body*, yet kept alive by the very latest scientific methods! Nothing like it in captivity! It talks, it sings, it eats, it drinks, it laughs, it cries like a lit-tle ba-a-a-by! The Bodiless Head sees all, knows all, tells all—and it never, never lies! See it right here at the incredible Congress of Wonders! See Little Big, the World's Smallest . . ."

As soon as Wanda Pearl has admitted Skinner—who, as usual, is funding the entire expedition—and his party to the tent, she jams a fresh butt in the corner of her mouth, fires it up, slaps her cash box shut, and rises from her table, wreathed in smoke. "Can it, Phil," she calls to the professor. "We've done got ten or twelve inside. Let's do a show."

"Right-o, pet," Professor Rexroat says obediently, breaking off in midspiel. "Any, ah, philanthropists among them, do you think?"

"Nah. That funny-lookin' duck with the sailor might be good for a few bucks. The rest is deadheads."

"Right-o," he says again. Wanda Pearl generally assumes, with his blessing, rather broad managerial responsibilities in Professor Rexroat's enterprises. Nonetheless, as he steps down from his podium, the professor adds, with a certain firmness in his tone belying the apology, "Ah, beg pardon, my lamb, but the fetch-it will be along shortly, and you know tonight is Friday, and on Friday nights after the show JoJo and I always enjoy a little taste of . . ."

"Oh, yeah," Wanda Pearl sighs, resigned. "And ever other damn night of the week besides. Y'know, Rexroat"—she opens the cash box and extends it to him—"if you don't make that morpho cut down on the 'shine and eat a little bite now and then, it ain't going to last you. It's as yeller as a Chinaman."

"Now, now," he purrs, helping himself to several bills (and an extra quarter for the fetch-it), "you know JoJo has her own little habits, lambie, even as you and I."

(Long ago and somewhat arbitrarily, Professor Rexroat had assigned his current Joseph/Josephine—latest in a long line of JoJos—the female gender, perhaps largely because, his old palship with Doc Woosley notwithstanding, he generally prefers the company of ladies. Wanda Pearl, however, noting the tiny, childlike, but undebatably male anatomical features among the peculiar assortment of charms the hermaphrodite exhibits at every show, is not quite prepared to certify JoJo as a member in good standing of the fair sex; she favors the nondenominational pronoun.)

"Well," she persists, "it's pretty near your whole show, the poor thing—it's your bearded lady and your talking head and your fortune-teller and your half-and-half—it's the only real square-up act you got, and you don't pay it nothing, hardly, and you make it sleep with the donkey, and . . ."

"Business, pet, strictly a business arrangement. And JoJo's needs are really very small, you know. She dines, I believe, quite satisfactorily on the midway."

"Yeah, outta the trash cans, poor little possum. Phil Rexroat, you ort to have your . . ."

But the professor has enjoyed a sufficiency of this examination of his business practices; he is already at the entryway to the tent. "Show time, dearest," he says, stepping inside. "You run along back to the trailer now, and slip into your little costume. You needn't worry your pretty little head about these trifles." He draws the curtain across the opening, and is gone.

"You ort to have your butt kicked," Wanda Pearl admonishes the curtain, "is what you ort to have." Then she flings her cigarette to the ground, tucks the cash box under her burly arm, and lumbers off around the corner of the tent, muttering vehemently under her breath.

5.

"Call that thing a meermaid?" Skinner Worthington snorts disdainfully. "I seen bigger tits on a sowbug. That damn kid . . ."

Skinner is peering into the murky urine-yellow depths of Miss Patagonia's formaldehyde beauty bath, in which Doc Woosley's shriveled dreamgirl floats serenely beneath her tiny horsehair wig. Sonny Capto is at Skinner's side; Wade is over at the far side of the tent, waiting in line to look through a microscope at the Lord's Prayer on a Pinhead, and the two Rosemarys are admiring, with many a shrill "Oooo, icksy," the ineffable allurements of the Chicken Boy.

"Yeah, she ain't sunk no ships lately, has she?" acknowledges the gunner's mate third class, scrutinizing the Patagonian Mermaid with an old salt's coolly appraising eye. "But hey, Skin, don't blame the kid. He was just goin' according to the picture outside. She looked fine, setting there on that rock. Maybe they had to shrink her to get her in the bottle."

But Skinner's one-track mind has already moved on to the next stop down the line. "Listen, Cap'n," he wheedles behind his hand, "howzabout we shake the kid and take these hides to the parkin' lot?"

"Aw, I don't know, Skin, beings as it's my last night and all, and I been promising Daddy all week long I'd . . ."

"Hey, c'mon! I got a pack of cundrums and a half-pint of sloe gin in the glove compartment—man, we'll tall-dog 'em, we'll thrill 'em and drill 'em! Here"—he fishes a small roll of bills from his pocket and peels off two singles—"slip him a couple of bucks for the rides, and tell him to catch a lift home with Burdette there. He'll be fine." Burdette Pence, the long-chinned fornicator with the vacant look who entered the tent earlier, is the hired hand on the farm next door to Wilbur Capto's. "Let's stay till the morphadyke comes on, though," Skinner adds, as Sonny, no slave to constancy, tucks the bills into his pocket. "I heard some of them at the poolroom say they seen one screw itself, one time. Them babes see a thing like that, they'll be all over us."

6.

Wade Capto, just stepping up to the Lord's Prayer on a Pinhead microscope, can't hear a word his brother and Skinner are saying, but he has caught them glancing at him out of the corners of their eyes, and as soon as he sees the two dollars disappear into Sonny's pocket, he understands perfectly the drift of their deliberations. ("The Lord give my good looks to Junior," runs Wilbur Capto's favorite family joke, "but he saved his mama's brains for Wade.") They're gonna pay me out, Wade tells himself bitterly, they're gonna pay me out and slip off with them two hoors. He wishes now that he hadn't seen the money change hands; then at least he could've pretended to himself that it was a real present—and from Sonny, not from Skinner Worthington. It'd suit Wade just fine if Skinner Worthington caught a social disease this very night, preferably a fatal one.

Not Sonny, though, please not Sonny. Every day Wade prays to God that Sonny won't catch a social disease, and that he won't get killed in a car wreck, and that he will come home from the war OK. There is much, very much, that Sonny Capto doesn't know and never will, but one thing he's got right as rain: his little brother thinks he hung the moon. Wade's and Sonny's mama—"the brainy one of all them Hurtle girls," everybody says—died of the childbed fever when Wade was born, and ever since Wade can remember, it seems as though he's had this worry in him, like an heirloom she'd entrusted to him, this little lump of fear that something bad would happen to Sonny, that Sonny's beauty wouldn't see him through. Wade loves his brother with a mother's love—and he fears for him as a mother fears.

The Lord's Prayer on a Pinhead turns out to be a gyp; you can tell right away that the words are printed inside the microscope somehow, and not on the pin at all. He won't count on the electric girl either, Wade resolves; if they'd mess with the Lord's Prayer, they'll mess with anything.

7.

Behind the tent, in the half-light from the midway, Wanda Pearl stumbles over the stake to which, during the off-hours when a show is not in progress, the professor tethers Little Big, the midget donkey who is in fact the only living nonhuman member of his menagerie. Cursing and grumbling, she moves on through the darkness toward the trailer until she comes upon what appears, in the shadowy lee of the back wall of the tent, to be a shapeless heap of rags among the trampled weeds. Wanda Pearl pauses and nudges it gently with her foot.

"Wake up, JoJo," she says. "Wake up, now. It's show time, hon, he'll be wanting you inside."

The heap stirs itself, whimpers, struggles to rise, an orderless form, vaguely human, draped head to foot in a chaos of greasy rags, the lower part of its face heavily veiled, its eyes as red-rimmed and bloodshot as open sores. As it rises, it is preceded by a powerful stench.

"Phew!" Wanda Pearl whistles softly. "Christ on a crutch, hon, you gotta quit sleepin' with that damn donkey!"

Even at its full height, she towers over this malodorous apparition, and she can feel those upturned mendicant eyes upon her face, beseeching her for what she cannot bring herself to give it, the merest touch of a human hand. Instead she says, "You scoot now, and check your talking head setup. After the show, maybe I'll fix you something good to eat."

"Hokay," it answers, in a cracked, androgynous little whisper, "hokay, missus." And it scuttles off into the shadows.

My sweet Jesus Christ on a crutch, Wanda Pearl says to herself as she mounts the steps to the trailer. If I had some ham I'd fix it ham and eggs, if I had any eggs.

8.

"... And now, my friends, allow me to direct your very kind attention to one of the most remarkable creatures that ever slithered out of the mudflats of the mighty Amazon onto the sunbaked sands of the Sudan, the Mammoth Three-Eyed Tasmanian Boa Constrictor"—the bottled and marinated reptile the professor indicates *is* a large one, and it does have three indisputably genuine eyes, all in a row and all its own; but it is rather less a Tasmanian boa from the mudflats of the Amazon than it is a cowsucker from a West Virginia corncrib—"captured on my last safari into the jungles of Borneo in the heart of darkest Madagasca-a-a-ar. . . ."

Professor Rexroat moves among his trophies and treasures, enlarging upon their histories and personal anomalies, his audience trailing raggedly in his wake. And when, at the glass redoubt of the Argus-eyed cowsucker, he pauses to describe how he and Momo, his trusty and devoted native bearer, bagged the monster just as it was preparing to sink its venomous sandwich-clamps into a particularly tasty portion of the beauteous number-one wife of a great Ethiopian Pygmy chieftain—thereby earning the professor the eternal gratitude and protection of all Ethiopian Pygmies everywhere—Skinner Worthington perceives a golden opportunity to advance the cause of romance, and seizes the moment.

Taking the two girls by the elbow and motioning to Sonny with a jerk of his head to come along, he steers them across the tent to the corner where Little Big, the World's Smallest Midget Donkey, is on display. Wade, noting the maneuver and suspecting at first that Skinner and Sonny are trying to sneak off without even paying him his two dollars, follows at a discreet distance.

The diminutive Little Big, a sleepy-eyed beast about the size of an Airedale, stands in his corner reflectively chewing his quid—dreaming, perhaps, of some colossal and gorgeous Shetland filly, for he sports an immense erection, gunmetal gray and dangling almost in the sawdust at his tiny hooves. Skinner, determinedly belaboring the obvious, urges the two nattering, tittering femmes fatales closer for a better look.

"Wouldja glim the boner on that little bastard!" he exclaims to Sonny out of the side of his mouth. "Them babes get a load of that, they'll . . ."

Disgusted, Wade tosses the remains of his candy apple to a grateful Little Big and turns away, and as he does he notices some small movement behind the old pink chenille bedspread that curtains off the opposite corner of the tent. Professor Rexroat, meanwhile, has moved on from the Three-Eyed Boa Constrictor to the Hairless Jackanape—in fact a stuffed armadillo with "Souvenir of El Paso, Texas" emblazoned on its underbelly—which, he solemnly avers, he and Momo subdued after a monumental struggle wherein the valiant Momo shed the last drop of his life's blood upon the jungle floor in the noble cause of the international advancement of science and human knowledge. Wade, hoping to catch an unauthorized glimpse of some rather less insensate Congress of Wonders phenomenon—even of Signorina Electra Spumoni herself, that fabled beauty!—eases around in back of the spellbound audience and lifts the curtain for a furtive peek.

Behind the bedspread, against the back wall of the tent, stands a low wooden shelf or table, which is bathed in wan, faintly viridescent light and seems somehow to float, legless, above the grassy floor. The table is laid with a scarlet sateen cloth with a gold fringe, and a large, silver-plated meat platter. And on the platter, all hairy and hideous in a pool of blood, is a human head, looking back at Wade with terrible, red-rimmed, all-seeing eyes. Their eyebeams meet, the head utters a tiny squeak of terror or surprise, Wade starts, drops the curtain, and as it falls he sees the head, as though it has opened its own throat and swallowed itself, disappear into a bottomless hole in the middle of the platter.

9.

In the trailer, Wanda Pearl sits before her mirror, putting on her Signorina Spumoni face. Through the open window behind her, she hears the hubbub of the midway, the distant piping of the carousel, the agonized greaseless creak of the Ferris wheel, and faintly, from within the tent, the professor's eulogy of his late associate Momo.

That old rip, Wanda Pearl muses fondly; he'll get more use out of a make-believe slave than most people would out of a real one.

She applies a final touch of crimson to her Kewpie-doll lips, smacks them noisily for the mirror, takes up her eyebrow pencil and haphazardly describes a pair of lopsided arches on her lowering brow. That the two new eyebrows look as if they belong on two different foreheads doesn't bother Wanda Pearl in the slightest, any more than it bothers her to go around on the street, sometimes, wearing one black shoe and one white shoe. If she was all that hipped on having things just so, she never would've hooked up with a pickled-punk show in the first place.

Poor little JoJo. The professor is always claiming there's no need to feel sorry for freaks—"because," according to him, "the worst has already happened to them, you see. And so they need not fear the Unknown, as other mortals must." Which you can't depend on nothing Rexroat says, Wanda Pearl reflects, dabbing rouge on a corduroy cheek; he's got the Gift of Gab and can't help it. But they've had half a dozen different JoJos down through the years—they billed them all as Joseph/Josephine, so they wouldn't have to repaint the banner—and some of them was real morphos and some was gaffs, and as far as Wanda Pearl is concerned they was all real pathetic. They just didn't know what they was, poor things.

Wanda Pearl halfway wishes she hadn't seen that sailor boy out there; he reminds her too much of Rodney, the boy she ran off from Oklahoma with, that got killed working on this very Ferris wheel ever so many long years ago. Rodney was the pretty-boy type himself, just like the sailor. He'd had a mean streak a yard across, the little sneak, but she had loved him anyhow, loved him and loved him. If that Ferris wheel hadn't broke down, and Rodney had lived, and her and him had stayed together till she'd had to kill him herself, the sneak, and they'd've had a little baby and it had been a boy, it would be a whole lot like that other kid by now, the sailor's little brother. Rodney Junior, she would've called it, and it would be the sweetest thing that ever drawed a breath.

The thought of Rodney Junior brings two fat tears welling to her eyes. As they course down her cheeks, tracing twin rivulets like snail tracks in the rouge and powder, she comforts herself with the certain knowledge that at least there ain't any little Rexroat Juniors running around loose, telling lies and keeping people all mixed up.

10.

"One of the most excessively edifying presentations in the entire field of scientific and educational entertainment ... eldest daughter of the maharaja of Marzipan ... refined and cultured to a high degree in the finest finishing schools on the European continent ... performing her internationally acclaimed Dance of the Seven Veils ..."

Now there sidles forth from behind the chenille bedspread a squalid, shapeless little hobo's bindle of tattered Gypsy finery and tinkling gaud, veiled and burnoosed like a Casbah houri, its thin, sallow arms bedizened in dime-store flash. Hiking up its sundry skirts and petticoats to expose dusty gray ankles in ancient, broken brogans without laces, the ragged figure parades its uncomely self up and down before the wondering audience in a small, sad parody of feminine allure until the professor announces that "without further ado, the Congress of Wonders proudly presents ... ," whereupon the specter turns its back and then turns round again with the veil stripped clean away, revealing a jaundiced, mercilessly pockmarked countenance, eyes as red as carbuncles, the features actually rather fine and delicate and not unwomanly, yet sporting—as indisputably its own as the Tasmanian boa's extra eye—a wispy mustache, like a dirty upper lip, and scant, goatlike chin whiskers. Wade Capto recognizes it right off; he'll be seeing those avid, feverish eyes in his nightmares.

"... proudly presents the lovely and talented JoJo, the unique, original, one and only Bearded Contessa of Lisbon—where all the Lisbians come from! And now, my friends, moving right along ..."

"Hold it right there, bub!" Skinner Worthington demands. "How do we know this here's a woman?"

"Old Skinner!" Sonny marvels at his partner's acuteness. "They don't get nothing past old Skinner!"

My brother, Wade mourns, is so dumb he thinks Skinner Worthington is sharp.

"Quite simple, m'boy," the professor is assuring Skinner. "Easy as throwing fish guts in the river, as the philosopher says. You must merely take our JoJo in your arms, a handsome young chap like yourself, take our JoJo in your arms and give her a *leetle* kiss, and—"

"Oh, pew!" wails Little Rosie. "Don't you dare kiss that old thing, Skinner Worthington, you might turn into one yore*self*!"

"—give her a nice little kiss, you see, and if she kisses back, she's a woman! But if *he* kisses back, why, then you've got yourself a man, don't you know!"

"Haw! Pucker up them lips, lover-boy!" urges Burdette Pence, with all the wit at his command, and a couple of other rustic Cupids volunteer similar incitements. And at last even the contessa herself—or himself, or itself—has something to say in regard to the proposal. "No-o-o-o!" the wretched creature keens, in a melancholy falsetto. "JoJo do not kees zeez porson!" The demurral occasions a fresh round of pleasantries at Skinner's expense, throughout which he stoutly disavows any such amatory pretensions, while the Bearded Contessa makes a hasty exit.

Wade's own sympathies are divided. Kissing Joseph/Josephine would be an awful prospect—but he believes he'd sooner kiss them both than Skinner Worthington.

"There she goes, the Bearded Contessa! But fear not, my

lovelorn Romeo"—this is addressed to Skinner, over his spirited disclaimer—"JoJo will return to our stage momentarily, and reveal to us the deepest secrets of the universe! The Human Enigma! Both halves fully capable of the sacred act of procreation! But first . . ."

11.

According to Professor Rexroat's reliably exhaustive introductory remarks, when Signorina Electra Spumoni's sainted mother, great with child, was struck down by a bolt of lightning at the midwife's very door, the central nervous system of the infant daughter pulled from the late mother's womb was discovered to have undergone a major rearrangement, leaving the child with AC red corpuscles and DC white corpuscles, thereby rendering her forever immune to the deleterious effects of electrical power. ("For God tempers the wind to the shorn lamb," the professor reminds his little flock, perhaps harkening back to some long-forgotten sermon delivered in this same tent when he was in a different line of work.) And so the signorina, having fled the old country before the jackboots of the tyrant Mussolini, has condescended to exhibit her remarkable capacities to the American public, strictly in the interest of the international advancement of science and human knowledge, with the clear understanding that all proceeds from these demonstrations be set aside for the establishment, back in her beloved homeland after the war, of a place of refuge for children orphaned by the conflict, with whom, naturally, she feels a special kinship.

Having said that much (and a good deal more), the professor stands aside and presents to his patrons' view, all the while reminding them that it is absolutely the Genuine Authentic Certified Simulated Regulation article, a large, bulky object shrouded beneath a profoundly soiled bedsheet. With a flourish, he whips aside the sheet to display a rough wooden armchair affixed with various straps, clamps, and metal plates—an exact working replica, he solemnly attests, of the principal item of furniture in the death house at Sing Sing. He then commends to their attention, mounted on a panel behind the chair, an elaborate electrical apparatus with an oversized, ominous-looking switch. This device, the professor avouches, will deliver "one *hun*-dred thousand deadly volts" of electric power into the mortal person of the chair's occupant—in this instance, happily, "the only living human being ever to survive an electrical charge of this stupendous magnitude, the scientific wonder of this and every other age, the very very lovely and talented Signorina Electra Spumoni!"

All these compliments notwithstanding, however, the phenomenon so described is still—as the vigilant Skinner Worthington is quick to observe, indignantly—"that big bucket-headed old bag we seen outside!" This despite the fact that she has somehow insinuated herself into a strapless, liver-colored sarong with a sequin-spangled lightning bolt spanning her bosom (and a pack of Raleighs peeking from her cleavage), her hams bound in torn black net stockings, her big number nines jammed into tiny white down-at-the-heels majorette boots with ratty gold tassels, and enough paint on her face to lay down a primer coat on a two-car garage, the whole ensemble topped off with a mangy oakum wig, like the pelt of one of Doc Woosley's famous leftovers, cocked pugnaciously on her beetled brow.

"Watch that mouth, rube," Signorina Ratliff snarls, glowering inhospitably at Skinner as she settles herself in the electric throne. "I'll smack the pee-waddin' outta you!"

"Kindly refrain," Professor Rexroat puts in hurriedly, "during this highly experimental procedure, from all remarks which might upset the delicate balance of the signorina's central nervous system . . ." As he delivers the admonition, the Man of Science is energetically lashing and clamping his subject into the hot seat—to restrain her, he hints, from rocketing through the roof of the tent when he lights her up.

"She ain't no damn Senior Rita!" Skinner protests. "She's just that big—"

"Better stow it, mate," Sonny cautions. "We wanna see the secret act of pokeration, don't we?"

"I'll pokerate *him*," Wanda Pearl vows, "the little—" But her malediction is cut short when the professor, cognizant of the tradition that holds that the show must go on and anxious, accordingly, to keep it proceeding apace, stops her mouth by inserting into that capacious orifice the business end of "a Common Ordinary Everyday Basic Conventional Household Lightbulb," and turning on the juice.

Now Wanda Pearl, at this moment, is seriously out of sorts. She's sick and goddamn tired of turning herself into a goddamn floor lamp four or five times a night for a bunch of goddamn hayseeds that wouldn't know good entertainment from a poke in the eye with a sharp stick. Also, these little pointy-toed boots is killing her corns, and she's sure her wig

has got cooties in it, the way it's itching her old head, and
Rexroat has pulled the straps on the chair too tight again and
pinched her arms black and blue. Plus, what with thinking
about Rodney and little Rodney Junior that never was and
then that smart-aleck snot calling her an old bag, her nerves
is giving her fits. Sorry as she feels, sometimes, for the poor
little JoJo, she's fed right up to here with freaks and geeks and
rubes and carnies, and sincerely wishes she had went into
some other line of work where she could've dealt with a better class of people.

"... Five *hun*-dred thousand deadly volts, my friends!
Enough to light up the entire midway of the World's Fair in
Chicawga, in the great state of Ill-oh-noise!"

The electricity—which is the static kind and don't hurt
a bit—would make Wanda Pearl's hair stand on end except
that, under the wig, her hair's still put up in pin curls; as it is,
it feels as if the pin curls are about to come ripping up
through the wig like innersprings in an old horsehair sofa.
And when she touches the tip of her tongue to the butt end of
the lightbulb, it tingles like a memory, and the bulb glows as
softly as a maiden's blush, as though she were having a ro-
mantic thought.

12.

By the time Professor Rexroat accomplishes the illumi-
nation of Signorina Electra, Wade is barely watching. He's
tuned in to Skinner Worthington, who in turn is talking in a
low voice to Burdette Pence. As before, Wade can't hear what
Skinner's saying, but as soon as he sees Burdette look over at
him and grin his big slack-jawed, half-wit grin, he knows

what's going on, all right: instead of riding home in style in the rumble seat of Skinner's roadster, with the moon flying high and the night air cool on his face and maybe even a sip or two of Skinner's sloe gin, just for practice, and Sonny right there in the front seat where Wade can keep an eye on him, Wade will be going home tonight in the back of Burdette's pickup truck, which he saw Burdette hauling hogs in this very morning.

While the professor is freeing the signorina from the chair's comfortless embrace, he decrees a standing offer of a one-hundred-dollar U.S. War Bond to the estate of anyone willing to duplicate her ordeal. Skinner Worthington instantly receives a small chorus of nominations from the floor and again declines the honor, emphatically if not very graciously. Wade seriously considers volunteering, figuring he could will his war bond to Sonny to help him get his start in life after the war. But Sonny would just cash it in and spend it on some old hoor, Wade reminds himself gloomily, and probably catch a social disease in the bargain.

Professor Rexroat, having reassembled the audience before the chenille bedspread, is delivering himself of a few brief remarks by way of introducing the next act, the lovely and talented Bodiless Head—which, behind the curtain, is once again resting on the silver platter, with the remainder of its remarkable person crouching beneath the table, hidden by an artfully positioned mirror. Wade, having caught this act before, hangs back to have a reproachful word with Signorina Ratliff-Spumoni, who is standing now, rubbing her wrists to get the circulation going.

"I thought you said they was a girl."

"She couldn't make it," says Wanda Pearl, with a shrug.

"I had to set in for her." He's Rodney Junior made over, she thinks—look at them eyes. She has half forgotten, for the moment, that Rodney Junior . . . never was.

"Yes," the boy presses her, "but you said—"

"Listen, bucko, y' got in free, didn't ya?" Suddenly and inexplicably, she is almost angry at him, at his innocence, his goddamn country dumbness. "Never mind what I said! It didn't cost you one damn penny, did it? So why don't you wise the hell up, fer crissakes!"

Even as the kid dejectedly slouches off to rejoin the others, Wanda Pearl is already wishing she hadn't blistered him that way. But my sweet Jesus P. Christ on a crutch (she marvels as she slips behind the curtain to help the Head get ready for its act), if he was looking for somebody to tell him the goddamn truth about things, why the hell would he come to a goddamn pickled-punk show?

13.

"Pew! Gag!" squeals Little Rosemary when the professor draws aside the curtain. "Gag a *maggot*!" Big Rosemary echoes, leaning over the rope to poke her monkey-on-a-stick perilously close to the baleful, baneful eyes of the Bodiless Head. "It's that old morphadyke agin!"

The Head, yellow as a boiled cabbage, resplendent now in a turban fashioned of a dirty dish towel with a ruby-red bicycle reflector affixed to it like a third eye, regards its admirers with a stare of abject, defenseless horror. If it had hands, it would hide its face in them.

"The Bodiless Head! A living miracle of modern medical science and good old Yankee know-how! Tell these fine folks, O Head, is it true that you can see into the future?"

"My . . . dee-vine . . . sign," rasps the Head, "eendo-cate . . . de few-tchoor . . . to me." Its speech is halting, mechanical, almost without inflection, as though it hasn't the foggiest notion what it is saying.

The professor turns to Skinner and the business at hand. "So how about it, my friend? Two bits, a measly twenty-five centavos, the first dime of which goes in toto to the Gold Star Mothers' Relief Fund, and this lovely and no doubt talented little lady here"—Little Rosie, hanging like a sash weight to Skinner's arm, encourages the extravagance with a wall-eyed gaze of deathless adoration—"this little lady here can ask the Head any question she desires! The innermost secrets of the human heart! Five trifling little nickels! Thank you, my friend"—Skinner is grumpy, but he coughs up the quar-ter—"the bereaved mothers of our fighting men will re-member you in their prayers tonight!" Professor Rexroat approaches the Head, bows deeply, and describes a sweeping arc of obeisance with his pith helmet. "Speak to us, O Head!" he implores. "Reveal to us the ancient wisdom of the spirit world! We beseech you!"

"I know . . . naw-theeng," the Head confesses miserably, in a voice like a clock running down, "egg-zept . . . de fact of . . . my igg-no-rantz-z-z."

"The Head knows all!" the professor promptly contra-dicts his oracle. "Ask it what you will, little lady."

Skinner, in the interest of getting his quarter's worth one way or another, propels Little Rosemary forward with a shove and an affectionate pat on her low-slung rump. "*Quit,* stoopit!" Little Rosie snaps. Then she leans over the rope till she is almost nose-to-nose with the Head and, as if she supposes its misfortunes have rendered it hard of hearing, shrieks full into its face, "AM! I! GONNA! GIT! RICH!?!"

For a moment the Head appears to ponder the matter, chewing its answer. "Haf-fing de . . . fewest wants-s-s," it declares at last, "I am . . . near-est . . . to de gods."

"What the hell does *that* mean?" demands Skinner, still mindful of the quarter this intelligence has cost him.

"Why, who has the fewest wants, my boy? The rich man, that's who! This little lady is going to be . . . rich! Fabulously wealthy! Rich as Croesus!"

"Oh, poot," scoffs Big Rosie. "She ain't got a winder to throw it out of."

"My . . . dee-vine . . . sign . . . ," the Head begins again, as Professor Rexroat closes the curtain on its act, "eendocate . . . de few-tchoor . . ."

14.

Professor Rexroat stands before the curtain extolling the divers charms and virtues of the Congress of Wonders' final presentation of the evening's entertainment, the international star of stage, screen, and radio, the lovely, talented, and delightfully versatile Joseph/Josephine, the Human Enigma. Wanda Pearl has put on her tattletale-gray dressing gown over her costume and returned to the electric chair, where she is resting her dogs and having a smoke. Wade Capto, meanwhile, has worked his way to the front of the crowd and is attending, rather skeptically at this point, to the professor's account of how Joseph was once employed by day as a palace guard in the court of the czar, while Josephine served as the Crown Prince Rasputin's favorite concubine at night.

"Is it gonna pokerate itself?" Skinner Worthington calls out, with a cackle.

"I'll pokerate *you!*" Wanda Pearl promises again, half rising from her chair. But the professor hastily assures Skinner that the Human Enigma is "fully capable of *all* the bodily functions," indeed that it positively *specializes* in the sacred act of self-pokeration—and that, in consideration of the enormous expense of maintaining this magnificent national treasure in the style to which it inevitably became accustomed during its years with the czar, the management has deemed it necessary to require the insignificant sum of fifty cents, additional, per patron of the arts, Hollywood talent scouts of course excepted, for each and every exhibition of the enigma's remarkable gifts. . . .

Wanda Pearl moves into the crowd—or what's left of it, after several impecunious types have departed, grumbling—to collect this final tribute to Professor Rexroat's powers of persuasion. A couple of elderly pensioners elect to stay ("I've lived in Burdock County eighty-two years," one of them quakes, "and I'll pay fifty cents to see any dern thing that don't come from around here"), and there's also a half-drunk plumber named Pipes Marquardt, who claims to be sticking around out of professional curiosity. Burdette Pence has sent his wife and daughter out, on the grounds that "hit might mark them babies," but he manages to locate fifty cents in the bottom of his snap purse to finance his own education.

"This goes to the Home for Old Morphadykes, I reckon," Skinner gripes, handing over two more dollars to

Wanda Pearl. "I don't have to pay for this here shit-heel, too, do I?"

He means Wade, who turns and glares at Skinner as if he'd like to kick him in the shins.

"Nope," says Wanda Pearl resolutely, with the professor, himself for once incredulous, looking on over her shoulder. "This boy don't need a ticket. He's too little, and he ain't a-watching it."

15.

Outside, Wanda Pearl resumes her seat at the card table, while Wade stands nearby, staring moodily at the happy throngs of revelers streaming past him. Wade's posture is mopish and sullen; he is still brooding over the insult he has suffered. Far off in the night sky, lightning flickers fitfully, like a bombardment in a distant war. Despite the warmth of the evening, Wanda Pearl shivers and draws her duster more closely about her.

"It's fixing to rain dishrags around here after while," she remarks, eyeing the sky warily. Signorina Electra's unique history notwithstanding, Wanda Pearl never did like lightning.

Great, Wade is thinking; rain would sure slow down the action in that rumble seat. Aloud, he says, in tones of deep aggrievement, "I don't see why you couldn't've let me stay and watch it. After I had brung in all those customers, I don't see— "

"Let that learn you a lesson, then," Wanda Pearl breaks in. "A shill is just the bait on somebody else's line. Ain't nothing lower than a goddam shill." She still sounds a little rougher than she means to—but she would've said the exact same thing to Rodney Junior, if he'd been there.

"It ain't even a real morphadyke anyhow, I bet," Wade sulks, consoling himself with a few sour grapes.

"Behold, the Human Enigma!" That's the professor, from the far side of the canvas wall just behind them. "Moments to witness, a lifetime to forget! Examine closely the—" Here the stentorian voice is drowned out by the screams and screeches of the two Rosies, carrying on as if their delicate sensibilities were being assaulted horribly.

"It's real enough, poor little booger," says Wanda Pearl, with a sigh.

"Well, it's a sorry-looking thing." That sounds ungenerous even to Wade, and right away he wishes he hadn't said it.

"Don't you be throwing off on that morphadyke," Wanda Pearl rebukes him, stomping out one Raleigh while fishing in her bodice for another. "It ain't had our advantages."

The Human Enigma has taken its final bow. Pipes Marquardt is first out of the tent, listing slightly and looking a little green around the gills. Then the two ancients totter into view, shaking their hoary heads in wonderment or dismay. "I went plumb to Orlando, Florida, and back in 1926," says the better-traveled of the pair, "but I never seen the beat of that." Next out is Burdette Pence, grinning hugely. As he passes Wade, he motions in the direction of the parking lot and says, "Air m'sheen's over h'yanner," which Wade, after a moment's consideration, understands to mean that the Pences' truck is over yonder.

Now Skinner and Sonny and the girls emerge, blinking in the sudden glare of the midway. Sonny's summer whites, as he approaches Wade, are dazzling, but his hat still graces the prow of the SS *Big Rosemary*.

"Listen, shipmate," he says, looking Wade not quite squarely in the eye, "me and Skin, we—"

"You all go on," Wade interrupts. "I'm ridin' home with Burdette." On Sonny's sleeve, just at the level of Wade's eyes, is his gunner's mate third class patch—two tiny silver cannons, crossed, on a field of white, with a single stripe below it. Wade studies it intently; the cannons swim in and out of focus like two little minnows in a jar.

"Well, here"—Sonny glances back to make sure Skinner isn't watching—"here's you something for the Tilt-A-Whirl and all." He fumbles with two fingers in the pocket of his blouse and extracts a dollar bill. Wade can see the outline of Skinner's other dollar—Sonny's now—still folded up in Sonny's pocket. Sonny holds the first bill out to him, but Wade doesn't reach for it.

"C'mon, Cap'n Capto!" Skinner calls. "These gals is ready for Freddy!"

Sonny stuffs the dollar in Wade's shirt pocket. "Wake me up early in the morning, shipmate, and we'll shoot us a few buckets before train time." Wade nods mutely, biting his lip. Sonny reaches out and squares the swabbie hat on Wade's brow, then steps back, snaps to attention, and throws him a stylish salute. "OK, sailor!" he barks. "Show us some *navy*!" Wade manages a listless salute in return and a mumbled "Aye, aye, sir." Sonny grins, dismisses him with an "At ease, shipmate!," and turns away.

"Let's *go*, you all!" Big Rosie pleads, grabbing Sonny's arm. "I hafta take a whiz!" Little Rosie pauses at the midway's edge to wipe her shoe in the grass. "Oh, shit," she laments, "I stepped in some doggy-do!" Skinner promises her a brand-new pair of saddles—wholesale price and no rationing stamps—and drags her off down the midway after the others.

"Them two young ladies," Wanda Pearl observes when they are gone, "is as common as pig tracks."

"Listen, ma'am," says Wade, with sudden urgency, "can I go back in and ast that Head thing a question?" He shows her Skinner's dollar. "I can pay, see? Just one question."

Wanda Pearl is touched; nobody's called her ma'am in the longest time. "Hon, that poor thing don't know nothing worth paying for," she tries to tell him. "Phil learnt it that stuff hisself, out of a book. Them sayings is by Socraits somebody, I don't know his last name."

"Well," the boy says stubbornly, "I gotta ast it something. It don't have to get back in its hole or nothing. I just . . . I just need to ast it something."

The little old rube's fixing to bubble up and cry, Wanda Pearl sees; his brother and that other squirt ort to have their butts kicked. "Well, hell," she says, "all right then, come on." At the entrance to the tent, she stops to say, a little less gruffly, "Put your money away, it might draw flies."

16.

The fetch-it has come and gone; Wade and Wanda Pearl find the professor standing before the closed chenille curtain, refreshing himself with a long pull at a pint bottle containing an elixir the approximate color of the Patagonian Mermaid's formaldehyde. The Human Enigma seems to have repaired

backstage, perhaps to set to rights whatever state of desha-
bille has resulted from its recent exertions.

"M'dear?" says Professor Rexroat, plugging his pint
with a stub of corncob. "To what do I owe—?"

Wanda Pearl brushes past him, saying, "You better lay
offa that jake-leg, Rexroat. Hard telling what all's in it. You
stay here," she orders Wade, and she disappears behind the
curtain.

"She's gonna let me ast that Head a question," Wade ex-
plains to the professor. "It's on something I need to find out
about."

"Of course, certainly, by all means. But as you will perhaps recall, there is a small, ah, gratuity connected with the
Head's, ah, oracular services, and—"

"Can that, Phil," Wanda Pearl instructs from out of
sight. "This one's on the house. You can open the curtain
now."

The professor raises his eyebrows, pockets his pint, and
does as he is told. The curtain drawn aside, the Bodiless
Head is as before, a ghastly, turbaned cabbage on a bloody
platter. Wanda Pearl stands off to one side, hands on her
hips, waiting.

"Speak to us, O Head!" the professor importunes, with a
perfunctory tip of his pith helmet and a considerably fore-
shortened rendition of his traditional deep salaam. "Tell us
what you see, tell us *all*!"

"I know . . . naw-theeng," the Head avers, inconsolably,
"egg-zcpt . . ."

"Never mind about that, O Bodiless One. Our young
friend here"—Wade steps to the rope and, for reasons that

are to remain forever mysterious to him, takes off his hat and bows his head—"our young friend desires to know . . ."

He defers to Wade, who hears himself say, in a voice scarcely above a whisper, "Is Sonny gonna make it through the war?"

"O-o-o-o-o . . . ," groans the Head. "O-o-o . . ." Out on the midway the Tilt-A-Whirl roars, the Ferris wheel creaks, the carousel tinkles, the barkers cry, the girls scream, and there is the rumble of distant thunder. But within the tent a terrible silence prevails while the Bodiless Head struggles to speak.

"O-o-o-o-kiiii-naaaa-waaaaaaaa!" the Head intones at last. "O-o-o-kiii-naaa-waaa!"

Wade looks to the professor for an interpretation and meets with a *no comprende* shrug; the Man of Letters purports to be as mystified as Wade is. And when Wade looks back, the Head is gone, withdrawn into its hole again. On the platter is the empty turban, a wadded dish towel in a pool of painted blood.

"That's all?" Wade asks in disbelief.

"That's it, son," says the professor, not unkindly. "That's the whole shit-a-ree, as it were."

"Well, it's all a big gyp, then."

"That's as may be," admits the professor, holding back the exit flap for him. "But you must never presume upon the cosmos, my lad. That wouldn't be . . . good policy."

"Aw, *bull!*" the boy flings back angrily as he rushes out. Through the opening they see him pause momentarily at the teeming midway's edge, like a reluctant swimmer on the bank of an arctic stream. Then he plunges in and is swept away.

"Awright, Phil Rexroat," Wanda Pearl demands to know, "how come the JoJo called that poor child a Okie? You ain't been learning it to throw off on the Okies, I hope."

"The word, my lamb," says the professor, in his most sonorous, funereal tones, "is Okinawa. It's ... a place in the war."

And he too exits through the flap.

The Human Enigma parts the ragged draperies that conceal the base of the Bodiless Head's hidey-hole and creeps fearfully into the light. As it labors to its feet, the professor, out front, cranks up his spiel for the next show.

"This way, this way, this way, this way! See the Pomeranian Humbug! See the Himalayan Quahog, World's Only Man-Eating Bivalve, Terror of the Andes! It's sensational, it's scientific, it's ..."

For a long moment, Wanda Pearl and JoJo stare wordlessly at each other across the narrow space between them. Then Wanda Pearl opens her arms and they embrace, each patting the other tenderly on the back, as grieving women will.

FINCH'S SONG: A SCHOOL BUS TRAGEDY

And . . . there came a stray sparrow, and swiftly flew
through the house, entering at one door and passing
out through another. As long as he is inside, he is not
buffeted by the winter's storm; but in the twinkling
of an eye the lull for him is over, and he speeds from
winter back to winter again, and is gone from
your sight.

So this life of man appeareth for a little time;
but what cometh after, or what went before, we
know not.

THE VENERABLE BEDE

SO HERE'S CLAUDE Craycraft standing in the doorway of Craycraft's Billiards on the courthouse square in Needmore on a hot late-summer afternoon in 1947, his triangle rack draped around his turkey neck like a wooden cowl. Claude is leaning against the door frame eating cherries from a brown paper sack, idly spitting the pits across the sidewalk at the windshield of his half-brother Clarence Fronk's '34 Plymouth coupe, when who does he spy coming up the street but Clarence himself—"Finch," as he is called—a loosely organized little bundle of tics and tremors and twitches inching along like a ten-cent windup toy, attempting (the yellow-bellied, knock-kneed, bald-headed, tongue-tied little shit-ass, Claude opines inwardly) to look over his shoulder with his right eye to make sure nothing sneaks up on him, while keeping his left eye fixed on the sidewalk at his feet in case the earth suddenly decides to open up and gulp him down.

Finch Fronk is a sick old man. Nothing new in that, of course, for he's been working up to it all his life. He's been a sick infant, a sick boy, a sick youth, a sick young man, and now at last he's a sick old man of twenty-eight and getting sicker (Finch tells anyone who can spare the time to hear him out) "b-by the god d-dern m-m-m-*min*ute!" Heart trouble, that's the problem. Finch was born as blue as a cobbler's thumb, and young Dr. Jibblet, who attended his arrival in this vale of sorrows, proffered the unhappy diagnosis manfully. "With this heart," prognosticated the youthful physician, his stethoscope still in his ears, "the poor little dinkus will never live to cast a vote." Yet the learned Dr. Jibblet has been in his grave for years, whereas the Poor Little Dinkus, although not exactly the picture of health, has already voted in four elections and is still thoroughly sensible to the pinch. If Claude Craycraft were a betting man—and in fact he does do a little bookmaking on the side—he'd lay odds that his half-brother will outlive him too.

Which really chaps Claude's ass. According to Claude's lights (those feeble glimmerings in the stygian gloom), if a person has enjoyed the benefits and advantages of being about to die all his goddamn life, he ought to have the goddamn common Christian decency to go ahead and do it. Hadn't Mommy went and bought Clarence that shiny red Electric Flyer wagon that time for Christmas, and then made Claude pull the puny little shit-ass around everywhere in it, so he wouldn't strain his little heart, till Claude got so sick and tired of it he had to leave home and go to shooting pool full time for a living? How about *Claude's* goddamn heart, he'd by god like to know!

As to that interesting mechanism, the heart of Claude

Craycraft, there has never been a soft spot anywhere inside it for his half-brother Clarence Fronk—nor, for that matter, for any person whatsoever of the slightest Fronkish extraction or inclination. Claude's own father, Dude Craycraft, a farmer—albeit an indifferent one, with an abiding passion for pool halls and beer joints and a concomitant distaste for family life—was killed in 1917 when in a moment of inebrious abandon, he attempted to go for an unauthorized joyride in his wife Maudie's rich Uncle Elrod's Essex automobile; unfortunately, Uncle Elrod had left the Essex in gear, and when Dude cranked it up, it promptly ran over him— which, in Uncle Elrod's oft-vented judgment, was good enough for the worthless son of a bitch. Claude was just sixteen when the Essex summarily executed its would-be abductor, but he'd already inherited Dude's affection for pool, as well as his aversion to all forms of physical exertion—as Maudie discovered when she asked him to be a pallbearer at his father's funeral and he begged off on the grounds that he'd hurt his back shooting pool the night before.

In all fairness to Uncle Elrod, by the way, we must add that when he expired in 1922, he bequeathed Claude the two thousand dollars that set up the enterprising lad in a poolroom of his own and made an ostensible man of him—although there were those Needmore skeptics who held that Elrod had made the bequest in a deathbed paroxysm of belated guilt—that indeed he'd seen Dude coming and had left the Essex in gear on purpose.

In any event, less than six months after Dude's hasty exit from our story, when his widow Maudie up and married Dude's longtime farmhand, a silent, plodding elderly German immigrant named Ott Fronk, it didn't disturb young

Claude at all at first. He figured that Maudie had seen the handwriting on the wall, as far as getting farmwork out of a pool shark was concerned, and had seized the opportunity to guarantee herself a free, full-time hewer of wood and drawer of water around the place. He was, in fact, pleasantly surprised that she'd shown so much initiative. And anyhow, he reasoned, the old Kraut was already pushing seventy, and he couldn't live forever, could he?

But then it turned out that the old Kraut *could* have lived forever, evidently, if he hadn't fallen from the top tier of the tobacco barn twenty-two years later in 1939, on his ninety-first birthday. And worse—far, far worse—a scant nine months after she and Ott were married, Maudie, at the unseemly age of forty-three, gave birth to the yellow-bellied, knock-kneed, bald-headed, tongue-tied little shit-ass Claude sees coming up the street this very minute.

And now Claude notices that right there in the gutter, in the shade of the automobile, slumbers his own aged but still resolutely lustful coonhound Delano—Claude is a Republican—sleeping off a long night's fruitless pursuit of a beagle bitch desperately in heat but too short for Delano to enjoy even if a dog had knees to get down on.

"Wuff!" Delano sleepily avers, as if to acknowledge his master's scrutiny. He rouses himself just long enough to administer a couple of quick slurps to his febrile, crimson member with a long pink tongue, then drops back off to beagle dreams again—but not before Claude recalls that he saw Finch petting that very beagle in the courthouse yard not an hour ago, while she, hungry for love wherever she could find it, wrapped herself ardently around and around Finch's pants leg. Claude grins; something is beginning to occur to him.

Moreover, chugging down the street toward the Billiards from the opposite direction is old Mrs. Turngate, the two-hundred-pound wife of the one-hundred-pound Lutheran preacher, a lady of legendary piety and propriety. At their present rate of progress, Claude calculates, she and Finch will reach the patch of sidewalk in front of the poolroom at just about exactly the same time. This here, Claude promises himself happily, is gonna be a good one.

"Hey, boys," he calls softly over his shoulder to the five or six loafers at the Billiards' bar behind him, "git a loada this!" The invitation is immediately rewarded by a gratifying little rush of patrons toward the front window. Even Pismire, the Billiards' old yellow tomcat, gets up and strolls lazily up the bar to see what's going on.

Meanwhile, Finch has eased over toward the curb to avoid getting himself run down by the fast-approaching Turngate Express. Claude pops another cherry into his mouth.

"*Say* there, baby brother," says Claude around the cherry, in tones so amiable they leave little invisible musical notes floating in the air around the words, "ain't that a dime yonder on the sidewalk?"

Finch is halted dead in his tracks by this unaccustomed display of affability. "Wh-wh-where at?" he demands, peering at his brother with unfraternal but perhaps forgivable suspicion.

"Why, right there in front of you!" Claude says sweetly. "Don't you see it, honey?"

"Wh-where?" Finch undertakes to ask again. Then avarice seizes him, and he bends way down and begins avidly searching the pavement for the illusory dime. And that's when Claude goes "Ptoo!" and sends the cherry pit whistling across Finch's bow and plinks old Delano on the beezer, hard enough to part his hair.

"WUFF!" Delano exclaims, more emphatically this time, struggling to his feet as fast as his old legs allow, with more than half a mind to deal severely with whoever perpetrated this outrage. But as he rises, Delano suddenly detects—Yes! Oh, yes!—the delectable redolence of *essence de la chienne* upon the air. Now his rheumy old eyes swim into focus, and there before him he espies not that sawed-off slut of a beagle but, tall as a French poodle, the nether portions of Finch Fronk, who is already in what must be, from a dog's point of view, the classic missionary position. With a joyous yelp and an alacrity that belies his years, Delano makes his move; in a trice he's halfway up Finch's back, humping ecstatically, with a huge grin on his chops and his tongue a-dangle out of the side of his mouth.

"JESUS CHRIST GOD ALMIGHTY!" Finch cries without a hint of a stammer, scrabbling across the pavement on all fours with Delano riding him like an incubus, the two of them scootching along at an extraordinary clip until Finch crashes, headlong but softly, into a pair of plump white columns that have inexplicably risen up right there in the middle of the sidewalk. Slowly, reluctantly, Finch's gaze travels upward over what seems to be a haystack-sized mound of monstrous purple orchids—actually Mrs. Turngate's floral-print summer frock—from the summit of which that reverend lady's stony visage glowers down as though she contemplates squashing him underfoot before he multiplies and infests the neighborhood. Even Delano is intimidated; he slides off Finch's back and slinks beneath the automobile.

"Clarence Fronk!" the old woman thunders. "What was that you said, mister?"

"Cheese 'n' crackers got all m-muddy?" Finch ventures wretchedly, in a small, stricken voice more prayerful than profane.

Mrs. Turngate is not mollified. "Of all the langwitch!" she admonishes. "Taking the Lord's name in vain right here on the public street! Have you been a-drinking?"

Finch is on his feet now but cringing and twitching so violently that there seems a fair possibility he'll simply shake himself to pieces on the spot, in a small explosion of springs and cogwheels and tiny parts of every description.

"Oh, n-nome!" he squeaks, wringing his little hands. "I don't dr-dr-dr . . ."

"Him and that dog's been hung up like that all afternoon, sister," Claude offers indolently from his doorway, to the very vocal satisfaction of the little audience behind him. "We was just fixing to take the hose to 'em."

"Well, I for one have never seen nothing so . . . so *crewd* and . . . and in*dig*nified in all my borned days!" declares the aggrieved matron, circling Finch as warily as Dives must have circled the leper at the gates of the Kingdom. "And him a school bus driver!" she flings back as she steams off down the sidewalk. "What a fine example to be a-setting for our yewth!"

Delano, noting that the coast has cleared, creeps into the light again and immediately begins sniffing at Finch's pants cuffs. Finch fetches him a kick in the slats that would've done him terrible damage if Finch had been a stronger man, and sends him scurrying.

"Sa-a-a-ay, Eleanor," drawls Claude, as he turns to go back inside, "when you and Delano has them pups, you be sure and save me one, hear?"

It ends—as it always has, as it always must—with Finch standing there awash in laughter and humiliation, the unutterable words beating against the backs of his teeth like birds in a cage, mutely entreating whatever gods might happen to be listening to grant him his heart's twin desires—for release, and for revenge.

——

The Yonder River, as those who live along its banks are fond of saying, is so crooked it's a wonder it doesn't screw itself into the ground. In fact, they say, the crookedness is what gave the river its name: one minute it's right here, the next it's over yonder.

On an eminence with a commanding view of what is surely one of the sorriest hillside farms in the entire Yonder valley—eighty-five or ninety steep exhausted acres, mostly haired over with briars and brush—roosts a ramshackle old farmhouse of weathered gray clapboard, staring out upon the blighted prospect before it through two blank uncurtained windows like baleful eyes. Between the windows is a screenless door from which depends, like a crooked tongue, a two-step wooden stoop, all that remains of what was once a nice front porch, before the present occupants tore it off and burned it for firewood, along with the picket fence that once enclosed the front yard. The little yard itself is a minefield of trash, garbage, slop, and offal of every description, populated by half a dozen quarrelsome gamecocks, tethered separately to various pieces of junk but nonetheless raucously disputatious amongst themselves, and a single pair of round-bodied, tiny-headed guinea hens scuttling hither and thither like a set of quotation marks trying frantically to punctuate the roosters' colloquy.

Behind the house is a lean-to henhouse, a tumbledown smokehouse, a hog pen constructed mainly of rusty corrugated iron barn roofing, a swaybacked old tobacco barn (with several missing panels of roofing, testifying to the primacy of the hogs), and a tilted privy, caught, as if by a candid camera, in the very act of lurching and reeling across the backyard from the barn to the house, drunk on its own fumes. A narrow gravel road passes close before the house, and beside the road is an equally tipsy mailbox, with the name "Skirvin" painted crooked and bleeding along its rusty flank.

This unprepossessing property, still known locally as the Old Craycraft Place despite the latter-day invasion of Fronks and Skirvins, constituted virtually the entire estate of the late Maudie Miggs Craycraft Fronk, who left this vale of tears in 1941, and her lamented husband Otto von Himmelheinz Fronkenheimer—Ott Fronk for convenience's sake—who preceded her by a matter of some eighteen months (though he'd no doubt be here still but for that one misstep in the top of the barn). Maudie left it all, lock, stock, and bedrock, to her youngest son Clarence—"so the pitiful little thing will have somewheres to hang his hat," said Maudie tremulously, in her final days. Remembering rich Uncle Elrod's generous bequest to Claude back in 1922 and taking into account the prosperous nature, these days, of the poolroom-and-bookmaking line—of which she'd never quite approved anyhow, just as she'd never quite approved of Claude's wife Marge, a mussy little snip who'd run off with an Electrolux salesman and left Maudie's only grandchild, Claude Elrod Jr., to be raised by a bunch of sots and souses in a derned old poolroom—she had endowed her elder son with a lovely full set of doilies crocheted by his Uncle Elrod's widow Opal, and otherwise omitted him altogether from her will. Which, we hardly need surmise, *really* chapped Claude's ass.

By late 1941, when Clarence came into the property, he had already cheated the Grim Reaper out of two years beyond his allotted span, an accomplishment he attributed to the fact that from the day of his birth, Maudie and Ott had allowed neither Dr. Jibblet nor any other physician to lay a finger on him, having apparently concluded that the principal business of the medical profession consisted of placing curses on the clientele. Claude, on the other hand, was satisfied that his half-brother's inconsiderate longevity was owed to the readiness of certain persons Claude could name if they weren't his own goddamn mommy to tamper with the laws of nature, which decreed that the eldest son got the whole goddamn works the way the good Lord intended it to be, by god.

Well, as we have seen, the Old Craycraft Place is no El Rancho Grande. But while Ott and Maudie were on the job, the fences were tight, the fencerows were clean, the outbuildings were snug, the stock was well tended, there were flowers in the yard and curtains at the windows. And for a time after Maudie's death, the Ladies Aid Society of the Zion Evangelical Methodist Church, where she had devoutly worshiped for more than sixty years, saw to it that Clarence's larder was stocked with pies and cakes and other delicacies from their own kitchens, and they badgered their husbands (as they had done for Maudie since Ott's passing) into keeping up with the work on the little farm. That winter, despite Pearl Harbor and the sudden distant rumble of the war, Clarence's neighbors did his milking and slopped his hog; in the spring they set his tobacco and planted his corn and put in a garden for him; in the summer they chopped out his tobacco and weeded the garden; in the fall they cut the tobacco and housed it and picked the corn and ground it and killed the hog and put up the meat and stripped the tobacco and took it to market for him.

And more and more every day, they grumbled about it among themselves. The war effort was in full swing by then, their sons were getting drafted, help was hard to come by. As might be supposed, their complaints found a sympathetic ear at Craycraft's Billiards.

"Why, hell," Claude would commiserate, no doubt eulogizing his uncooperatively durable late stepfather as well as his seemingly immortal half-brother, "if me and you was Fronks and never done nothing but lay up in the bed till noon every day, we might live forever too!"

And to tell the truth, in those days, Clarence *was* enjoying himself a bit more overtly, perhaps, than was prudent, given his circumstances. Without Maudie clucking and wringing her hands over him all the time, he found that he could sometimes go for hours at a stretch without thinking about his imminent demise. He didn't sleep till noon, true, but all too often he came out of the house, yawning and stretching, at eight-thirty or nine to discover some disgruntled neighbor laboring away in his garden or his tobacco patch. A few times he went down and sat under a nearby shade tree and tried to keep that day's Good Samaritan company—it seemed to him the least that he could do—but they were usually in such a bad mood that he finally decided they were all prejudiced against people who stuttered, and anyhow, watching them work gave him nervous palpitations of the heart, so mostly he steered clear of them. He spent a lot of time down at the river, fishing—though the sight of fish guts upset his stomach, so one of the neighbors had to clean them for him. In the heat of the afternoon, he'd generally get in Ott's old Plymouth coupe and drive slowly around the countryside, to cool himself so he wouldn't get the heatstroke. Often, he'd drop by Claude's poolroom for a nice cold bottle of beer, to calm his nerves.

"We-e-e-ellll!" Claude would greet him. "If it ain't John D.! Would you keer for a cocktail, Mr. Rockyfella? I see you ain't died today, Mr. Vandybilt!"

Clarence, surprisingly, was not at all disturbed by these affronts. Indeed, his half-brother's bitterness confirmed, in a certain sort of a way, Clarence's own victory and was therefore even rather gratifying.

Yet who are we to say that Claude's case against his brother had no merit? It takes one to know one, goes the adage, and the failings Claude charged Clarence with— cowardice, self-pity, sloth, and an insufficiency of brotherly love—were certainly ones that Claude should have recognized on sight. What if Doc Jibblet had it wrong, what if all of Clarence's forebodings were unfounded? It was true, when you came right down to it, that his heart had never really *pained* him. But other men's hearts didn't go pittypat-*whup*, pittypat-*whup* inside their chests when they was laying up in the bed of a night, trying to get theirself a little sleep, other men's hearts didn't flip-flap around sometimes like a chicken with its head off, or jump into their throat every time anybody said boo to them, other men's hearts didn't leak and drip and gurgle so loud you could hear it clear across the room. ("That ain't your heart, that's your damn stummick!" Claude had hooted, the one time Clarence had ventured to call the phenomenon to his attention.) Oh, he was a sick man all right, sick as a poisoned crow. But was his ailment seated in his breast, or was it—Claude's diagnosis—all in his goddamn mind? We have nothing to fear, the president had once assured the nation, but fear itself. Clarence could have told the president, in no uncertain terms, that fear is more than enough to be afraid of.

Most evenings Clarence spent at home, listening to the radio—he started with *Lum 'n' Abner* at five o'clock and listened straight through *Moon River*, which came on at midnight—but a couple of nights a month he'd get back in the Plymouth after his supper and drive to Limestone, twenty miles away in the next county, where, in a little shotgun house down by the railroad tracks, there lived a lady named Mrs. J. T. Mooney, whose husband, Mr. Mooney, had a bad case of the TB. After she got Mr. Mooney settled for the night, Mrs. Mooney would raise the shade in the sitting room window, as an all-clear signal, and if you pulled up out front and tooted the horn, Mrs. Mooney would come out and, for two dollars, take a little ride with you. Clarence figured Mrs. Mooney was real good for his nerves; he even got to thinking that if he outlasted Mr. Mooney—as was beginning to seem, to his amazement, not just possible but probable—he might consider offering Mrs. Mooney the opportunity to become a citizen of Burdock County and an honest woman again.

But the bubble was about to burst. For on the day after

Christmas of 1942, Clarence received a letter that began "Greetings from the President of the United States..." He'd been drafted!

Not that he was worried; his heart, that sore but steadfast organ that had so often stood between him and a hostile world, would certainly protect him this time. The notice did mean, though, that he'd have to take the physical and submit his delicate interior to the prying scrutiny of the U.S. Army, and he feared the army doctors might renew Doc Jibblet's ancient malediction. Then he recalled, not without a certain niggling satisfaction, that his old nemesis was already the *late* Doc Jibblet, and it occurred to him that he might possess a little maledictory power of his own. If the U.S. Army intended to win this war, he told himself darkly, maybe they'd just better not mess with Clarence F-F-Fronk.

They held the physical over in Toomes County, in the Mount Ararat High School gym, which had been designated an Official Temporary Preinduction Examination Center. To get the local draftees to their appointment with destiny, the government had hired a Burdock County school bus and its operator, who happened to be Clarence's quasi nephew and Claude's only offspring, a rather dense young man named Claude Elrod Craycraft Jr.—Buster, they called him—who would himself be taking the physical. Buster had volunteered for the draft, not out of patriotism (as the father of three with a fourth on the way, he was entitled to an automatic deferment) but because he was married to a fat, mean, ugly woman fifteen years his senior, who seemed bent on surrounding him with fat, mean, ugly children, from the entire lot of whom the war would be a welcome respite.

The bus ride to Mount Ararat was a rough one for Clarence—an endless hour jouncing along the back roads in the close confines of a school bus packed with thirty-five or forty other young men (Clarence, remember, is at this time only twenty-three himself, though he looks twice that and carries himself like an octogenarian), mere boys, many of them, preparing to set out on the first great adventure of their lives. Those who passed the physical would have another twenty-one days to get their affairs in order, but that meant twenty-one days of fond farewells, twenty-one days of being petted and pampered and adored. Soon they would go marching off to war; women would swoon, children would throw flowers; soon they would be heroes, lovers, killers; soon they would be men.

So they were excited—nay, they were beside themselves, half-crazed with a volatile admixture of eagerness and apprehension, anticipation and regret, fear and valor; they were *wild*, as rowdy and raucous as a pack of schoolboys.

Naturally, they took it out on Clarence; they mocked his stammer and called him "Heartaches," they grabbed his hat and tossed it around and threatened to pee in it and throw it out the window, and then they *did* pee in it and throw it out the window, and one great hulking fellow administered a stimulating Dutch rub to Clarence's downy little skull for good measure, claiming it would grow hair. And the driver, his own nephew Buster, enthusiastically encouraged their depredations. "Pants him, boys!" Buster kept calling over his shoulder. "Pants that little booger!" And they *did* pants the little booger and wouldn't give him back his trousers till they'd passed the Mount Ararat city limits sign, and by then they'd tied the pants legs together and pulled all the buttons off the fly. Clarence tried to maintain his dignity and stay above it all, but it wasn't easy. It'd serve them right, in Clarence's opinion, if he just hauled off and had a heart at-t-t-tack right then and there.

Outside the gym were parked eight or nine other school buses from adjoining and nearby counties, and inside they found perhaps as many as three hundred naked men, each with a handful of papers and a little canvas bag of personal effects around his neck, some sitting in the bleachers filling out forms, some milling aimlessly about the basketball court, some shuffling around in little squads under the hectoring commands of a score of officious corporals who seemed to be everywhere at once, like sheepdogs working a newly sheared herd. Almost immediately, Clarence was naked, with his little coin purse and his daddy's pocket watch in a bag around his neck and any number of corporals nipping at his heels.

"*Awright, ladies, take it off! Drop your jocks and show your cocks! Now milk it down, milk it down, milk them peckers down, you got a drip, the corporal wants to see it! Move it out now, move it out! Awright, bend over, bend over, spread 'em, spread 'em, you got a asshole, the corporal wants to see it! Now cough, c'mon, cough, goddamn it, cough for the corporal, he's doin' you a favor, who else is gonna feel yer nuts? Awright, move it, move it, don't you know there's a goddamn war on? Up on the scale, hurry it up, move it, what the hell's the matter with you people, move along, move a—Jeezis Kee-reist, corporal, wouldja look at this here little plucked dicky-bird here, a hunnert and six poundsa chickenshit, look at 'im shake and shiver, let's feed 'im to the Japs! Awright, Shorty, move it out, move it out, don't you know there's a goddamn . . ."*

At the blood-test station, the man in front of Clarence— who chanced to be his kinsman Buster—fainted dead away at the sight of his own blood. But when it was Clarence's turn, he stepped right over his prone nephew and held out his arm and shed his heart's blood like a natural man, watched it surge into a syringe the size of a water tumbler without a blink or a tremor—possibly because he'd looked ahead and seen that at the next station there was a corporal with a stethoscope, and he knew that when he got there, his ordeal would soon be over.

" 'Kay, ya toids, let's check dem tickers!" This corporal apparently hailed from Brooklyn; he sounded exactly like Harrington on *Mr. District Attorney*. "Hey, cheez, lissen t' dat, dis one really *does* tick!"

"That's Daddy's w-watch."

"Oh, yeh, I got yez on yer goodies dere, din't I! 'Kay, here we go"—now the stethoscope was on Clarence's breastbone, cold as the barrel of a gun—"hey, dat's betta, dat's betta, sound as a dolla, ya got yerself a reggala Gene Kruper in dere, 'kay, next man, next man!"

"B-b-b-but—"

"C'mon, Shortcake, 'fya can't talk, shake a boosh! Move along, move along, ya got a beef, take it to da koinel, he's da doc! Move it on out now, don't you know dere's a war on?"

Dazed, Clarence stumbled on toward the next station, where they were checking for flat feet. Behind him, he heard the revivified Buster ask the Brooklyn corporal, "You mean he ain't . . . ?" But Clarence—moving it on out, as ordered—was too far away to hear the rest of the question or the corporal's answer:

"Hey, man, I ain't no fuckin' heart expoit, I'm a goddamn cloik-typist! Da reggala heart guy had da shits dis morning. Dis is da goddamn U.S. Army, man, one guy can't do it, da next guy does! 'Kay, let's hear dat ticker dere, dat's it, sound as a dolla, move along, move it on out! ..."

But Clarence couldn't hear the Brooklyn corporal; what he was hearing instead at that moment was the flat-feet corporal, screaming, "Fer crissakes, lookit them tootsies! What the hell are you, bub, a goddamn duck? Jeezis Kee-reist"— he grabbed Clarence's papers out of his hand, smacked them down on his table, slashed a check mark beside the "flat feet" designation, scooped up a rubber stamp and slammed an ink pad so hard with it that droplets of ink flew out as if he'd smashed some large, black-blooded insect, then slammed the stamp down on the topmost paper with even greater force, and thrust the whole stack back at Clarence with the word "REJECTED" emblazoned across it in inch-tall letters— "where in the hell do these hayseed draft boards find these goddamn misfits? Get your clothes on and get the hell outta here, Donald Duck, go set it in the goddamn bus!"

"B-but the ker-ker-ker ..."

"C'mon, gizzard-lips, spit it out! The colonel's a busy man, he ain't got time to waste on no goddamn 4-F, he's got twenty-five able-bodied men tryin' t' talk him into givin' 'em what you just got without even askin'! Move it out, move it out! Next man, next man, next man! Ain't you people heard there's a goddamn war on?"

"Hey, unk!" Buster chortled after him as Clarence tottered off in search of his clothes. "Dad's gonna be *quite* tickled to hear you ain't sick!"

During the bus ride home to Needmore, the Burdock County warriors-to-be were a good deal more subdued than they had been that morning, evidently having found their initial experience of military life surprisingly humbling. All of them had passed the physical save one grossly obese young man, one half-blind young man, and Clarence; and if any one of those three unfortunates could have read the thoughts of his fellow passengers, he might have discovered that for the first time in his young life, he was more envied than pitied or despised.

But even if Clarence were entertaining any such speculations, he would have taken very little solace from them. He rode home huddled in the rearmost seat of the bus, alone with his own unhappy thoughts. If he didn't have heart trouble, then what *was* that thing beating itself to death against his rib cage? What was it that spoiled his appetite and ruined his digestion and stopped his breath in his throat and woke him up with night sweats? How come his nerves was all the time shot plumb to billy hell? If he didn't have heart trouble, then who the hell *did*, he'd by god like to know!

Yet who would ever believe him now? He longed powerfully for the sweet, consoling, costly embrace of Mrs. Mooney, but at the same time he understood that he must never know that brief ecstasy again; it was too dangerous, he had to take care of himself, because who else would? No more cold beer, either; he had to keep his wits about him now. He was in peril every minute, everything was about to change, his trials were just beginning!

And in that, at least, he was dead right. Within a very few minutes after the bus arrived in Needmore, Buster Craycraft was in deep consultation with Claude, back by the pissery in Craycraft's Billiards, and already Claude had what he liked best: a scheme. Pismire, eyeing his master from his vantage point on the bar, knew Claude for a soul mate at a glance, for his master was grinning like the celebrated feline that had just swallowed the canary—beak, birdsong, and tail feathers.

Clarence was awakened the next morning by the bawling of his milk cow, Maybelle, standing in her stall in the
barn, unmilked and decidedly out of sorts. According to
Daddy's watch (which Clarence kept under his pillow at
night, for company), it was twenty-five till nine. *What's the
matter with people nowadays?* he thought irritably. Then he
remembered, and despaired. The word was out.

Needless to say, Clarence was not a practiced milker; it
was nearly noon by the time he got Maybelle to agree to go
back to the pasture—and by then she'd already shown her
displeasure by kicking over the milk bucket, unburdening
herself of a cow pie on his knee, and clubbing him several
times in the back of the head with her tail, which was full of
burrs and dried manure and as hard as a hoe handle. Wearily,
Clarence slogged back to the house and threw himself on his
bed again, and fell asleep with a desperate prayer that the
neighbor who'd been milking for him in the evening would
show up. But when he awoke at four-thirty, Maybelle was
back in the barn, bawling—and no sign of the neighbor. It
was pitch-dark before she let him leave the barn this time,
and he'd missed *Lum 'n' Abner* and *Just Plain Bill* and all his
other early evening favorites. And he had to fix himself a can
of pork and beans for supper; the Ladies Aid Society had
thrown him over too.

After three days of Clarence's inept attentions, Maybelle
came down with mastitis. "You ain't been getting her
stripped out," Pillbox Foxx, the veterinarian, said disgust-
edly after he'd looked her over. "You ort to let her go." Mean-
ing, Clarence knew, that Pillbox regarded him as unfit to

own a good milk cow. So Clarence called his neighbor, a man named Kinchlow—the very neighbor who had failed to turn up for the morning milking three days ago!—and Kinchlow came and after treating Clarence to yet another unspoken display of withering contempt, said, Yeah, he reckoned he could take her off his hands, Clarence being so busy and all—and offered him half what she'd have been worth three days ago! As they were loading Maybelle into Kinchlow's truck, Clarence couldn't stop himself from asking if Mizriz Kinchlow was making any of those good banana cream pies of hers lately. And Kinchlow said, No, by god, she wasn't, and if she was they'd be eating it theirselves, because sugar was rationed and bananas was hard to come by, and didn't he know there was a goddamn war on?

Clarence had to spend most of what he got for Maybelle to pay Pillbox's fee, and his little bank account was already running low. His dab of tobacco money was almost gone, mostly by way of certain bonuses that had been extracted from him by the blandishments of the winsome Mrs. Mooney. Moreover, that alluring creature had revealed, back at hog-killing time, an overweening passion for a bit of pork now and then and had subsequently acquired, in the form of little gifts of hams and chops and bacon, most of Clarence's hog. Indeed, all that he had left was a jar of pickled pig's feet, which Mrs. M. didn't particularly care for.

Still, he held out for another week, subsisting principally on pork and beans and black coffee and baloney sandwiches. But on the fifth day, the weather turned malevolently colder, just as he got down to his last few sticks of firewood. He huddled in bed for two more days, under a mountain of blankets, quilts, dirty clothes, Maudie's old winter coat, Ott's old bib overalls, and Maudie's hand-hooked rag rug off the sitting room floor; he even took her lace curtains out of the front windows and piled them on. Then, on the seventh morning, a Saturday, he opened his last can of pork and beans and found the contents frozen solid. He took the jar of pickled pig's feet back to bed and ate as much of it as he could stand, to build up his strength a little, and then got up and went outside and tried, hopelessly, to start the Plymouth, as he had done yesterday and the day before. It wouldn't start, of course, so he waited there till he saw, far upriver, the mailman's car working its halting way along the river road; then he left the Plymouth and stood by the mailbox, shivering violently in the spitting snow, till the mailman got there and grudgingly agreed to give him a ride to town.

It being a blustery midwinter Saturday morning, the Billiards was already full of noise and smoke and farmers, but when Clarence came scuttling in out of the cold, it was like in the westerns when the Fastest Gun comes striding through those swingin' doors: you could've heard a pin drop.

"Why, as I live and breathe!" exclaimed Claude, as the beer drinkers at the bar grinned and nudged and snickered expectantly. "If it ain't the Duker Windsor! I figgered you was liable to show up any day now. So what brings you to town, baby brother? Your money crowd you out of the house, did it?"

"I—I need somewheres to st-st-stay, big b-brother. I ain't got no heat out at the p-p-place. I was thinkin' ab-b-b-bout that r-r-r-r-..."

"You was thinkin' about that nice little room I got upstairs here, I'll just bet! Why, yes indeedy, you can move right in, baby brother! Glad to have you!"

"Well, how much would you ch-ch-ch-ch-...?"

"Charge you? Why, not one penny, sweetheart, not one penny! But I tell you what, I been needing me somebody to clean my spittoons and swab down the pissery of an evening, and rack balls for me when it gets busy in here of a Saturday afternoon and all. Now you take on them little chores for me, honey, and I'll let you have that room absolutely free of charge. How's *that*, by god! And don't you thank me for it, neither! Because, you know, what's a brother for?"

Clarence could only gulp and nod in acquiescence, but he was horrified. What about his weak stomach? And that thought reminded him of another, even more pressing question: "B-Big brother, where'll I eat at?"

"Well, sir," said Claude, with an air of vast magnanimity, "I been studying about that too, and I have done come up with a leet-tle plan. Because I would hate to have to see you go to the county poorhouse—it might reflect bad on the family name, and all. But before we get into that, Waldo there"— he indicated the far end of the bar, where a notorious sot named Waldo Skirvin languished facedown in a pool of spilled beer—"Waldo there had him a little accident back in the pissery a while ago, he kinda throwed up a little. So maybe you wouldn't mind . . ." Claude reached under the counter and came up with a bucket and a mop, "Now don't you rush yourself, honey. You got all the time in the world, all the time in the world."

Clarence trudged off to his work, numberless days of spittoons and little accidents before him, pickled pig's feet already roiling in his innards.

When he emerged from the pissery twenty minutes later, pale as moonlight, he was greeted with a ragged but rousingly derisive little cheer from the barflies up front, but he barely heard it. Filled with dread—what further raptures might his brother have in store for him?—he staggered forth to meet his fate.

"Now then," Claude said, leaning over the bar as if to speak to Clarence in the strictest confidence, yet talking loud enough that everyone in the place save the comatose Mr. Skirvin could hear his every word, "now then, where was we? I believe you was saying something about . . . eating?"

N-not right now, Clarence said, with a shudder; no time soon.

Well, anyhow, Claude went on, when it's breakfast you want, we got pickled eggs right here—he directed Clarence's attention to a gallon jar full of sallow ovals floating in a bilious yellow fluid—which ain't but fifteen cents apiece, and crackers throwed in free. And when you want your dinner, there's you a big selection of all the finest candy bars and Nabs right there, a nickel apiece. Comes to supper, it ain't a better bowl of chili anywheres in Burdock County than they got down the street at the White Manor Café. But it takes money, bud, it all takes money.

Clarence couldn't argue with that—and he declined to try.

So, Claude explained, here Clarence was with a farm he couldn't use, and here was Claude's son Buster with a school bus *he* couldn't use, beings as he was about to go off and win the goddamn war. But as it happened, that school bus wasn't really Buster's, it was Claude's, because it was Claude which had put up the money for it and which had went to the school board and got the boy the route and the contract in the first place. So it was by god Claude's bus to do with as he seen fit. And what he seen fit was, he would just trade Clarence even up, one little old piddly-ass worthless scrap of a raggledy-ass farm for one good-running nearly brand-new two-year-old Reo school bus, and he would throw in, abso-by-god-lutely free of charge, whatever it had cost him under the table to buy Buster the goddamn route from the school board in the goddamn first place, and how was *that* for a goddamn deal?

B-b-but, big brother, Clarence managed to inquire, what do you *want* with the farm?

Well, said Claude, Gene Kinchlow had run old Waldo there off his place after Waldo got drunk and set Gene's tenant house afire. (Waldo raised his head just long enough to grin in modest acknowledgment of the distinction, before his forehead hit the bar again.) So, Claude went on, he thought he'd just let the Skirvins have the farm, to crop on shares. Then too, he'd been looking around for somewheres outside the city limits where him and a few of the boys could have theirselfs a little friendly cockfight or shoot some craps now and then of a Sunday afternoon (from the barflies came a murmur of appreciation for Claude's civic-mindedness), and that old barn out there would be just the ticket.

"But here's the size of it, baby brother," Claude continued, speaking mildly at first but with growing vehemence as he drove home his point, "a thing that's mine, I just naturally want to get my hands on it, see, I mean that's just the kind of hairpin I *am*, by god! If it ain't mine I don't want nothing whatsoever to do with it, hardly. But if it's mine, I *want* it, you see! And that farm was handed down to me by my goddamn anchesters, or ort to been, by god, and it's *mine*, and I mean to *have* the son of a bitch!"

There was an assenting thunk of beer bottles all along the bar; you couldn't fool this jury, they knew justice when they saw it, yes, by god! Clarence reeled back from the bar a step or two, looking wildly from one impassive face to the next, and appealed to the room at large, "B-but what if I . . . I mean, all them little ch-*chil*dren!"

"Pshaw," said Claude lightly, "it ain't a man in Burdock County as precautious of hisself as you are, baby brother. Them childring couldn't be safer if they was in their mommy's arms."

There was just one thing left for Clarence to say—part plea, part threat, part promise—and at last he forced himself to say it: "I . . . I'll d-*die!*" he cried.

Now there arose from his bar stool a tall, skinny, dour old retired barber named Geezer Wirtschaffner, who had cut Clarence's delicate little curls once a month until they'd all but disappeared when he was in his teens. For a moment, as this venerable sage approached him, Clarence supposed that here at last was the friend and defender he so desperately required. Geezer stopped before him, towering, worked an immense chew of tobacco here and there inside his mouth to clear his wise old tongue for speaking, then reached down and, with a long forefinger as rigid as an arrow, jabbed Clarence on the breastbone hard, just above the heart, and said, "Clarence, my boy, you ain't dead *yet!*"

———

On the following afternoon, Sunday, Clarence and Buster and Buster's best friend Chick Greevey, who hauled dead livestock for the fertilizer company in Limestone, moved Clarence's meager belongings from the homeplace to the room above the Billiards. It didn't take long. There was just Clarence's little bed—an iron World War I army surplus cot he'd slept on since he was five—and all those bedclothes, and a few clothes of his own, and a wooden kitchen chair, and a small, framed snapshot of Ott and Maudie on the courthouse steps on their wedding day, Maudie smiling uncertainly beneath a cloche hat scarcely bigger than a walnut shell, Ott looming and somber behind a shaggy walrus mustache the size of a pitchforkful of hay. They used Chick's malodorous truck, the dead wagon, for the move, and every night for months afterward Clarence shared his bed with the faint but inextinguishable stench of death clinging to the bedding.

Monday morning, with Buster riding shotgun to show him the route—which happened to be the river road, the crookedest, narrowest, meanest, most hellish twelve miles of unpaved perversity in Burdock County, the very road that passed before the homeplace—Clarence took his first turn at the wheel. Among the stops was Buster's own house (actually his mother-in-law's house, which Buster and his wife, Iota, and their several fat, mean, ugly children generously shared with her), where they picked up Buster's eldest, a corpulent third-grader named Clayton, known to his intimates as Clabber, who climbed into the bus and, to the vast amusement of his amiable parent, immediately smacked his Great-half-uncle Clarence on the back of the head hard enough to make the poor man bite his tongue. It was the first installment of a ritual that would be unfailingly repeated every school day, morning and evening, for all the ensuing years of Clarence's life.

Clarence never had a chance. From the very first day his passengers were utterly out of control, his bus a self-contained tumult and chaos, a rolling anarchy, hell on wheels. The little lambs fought and swore like drunken sailors, they beat each other over the head with schoolbooks and lunchboxes, the older boys smoked cigarettes and chewed tobacco and spit on the floor and boldly felt up the squealing girls, the younger ones threw up in the aisles and peed out the window, they carved "Fronk You" in the leather seat cushions and then pulled the stuffing out and piled it in the aisle and set fire to it, they pelted Clarence's hunched shoulders with whatever came to hand, spitballs and marbles and apple cores and artgum erasers—and one afternoon, in his sixth or seventh week as driver, he glanced in the rearview and saw to his horror a great brute of a boy named Harry Tom Powers creeping up the aisle behind him with what appeared to be an immense drop of some pale, viscous fluid dangling from his paw, and an instant later there came crashing down on Clarence's battered skull a Trojan filled with half a pint of buttermilk. The school bus lurched into the ditch and stalled.

"I'll *die!*" the children sitting nearest heard their driver vow, as he wiped the whey and thin, white shreds of rubber from his eyes. "I swear to god I'll d-die, I *will*, by god!"

And he just might have done it, too; he just might've clenched his jaw and gnashed his teeth and held his breath and sweated and strained until, b-by god, he *did* succeed in willing himself a heart attack. But at least for the time being, the will to live triumphed over the will to die—and so he lived, and didn't die.

It was along about this time that he acquired the trait that, in turn, brought him the nickname that was to stay with him the rest of his days. For so insistent had become his habit of glancing fearfully over his right shoulder, to see what mischief his darlings might be up to next, that the gesture had joined his nervous little repertoire of tics and twitches, a quick, mechanical, sidelong hitch of the head every ten seconds or so during all his waking hours. In the poolroom, some imaginative wag speculated that Clarence had lately been visited by an invisible little bird, which had perched on his right shoulder and was with him always, and that he turned his head time after time in order to hear its tiny song. In honor of the bird, they named him Finch, and like the bird itself, the name never went away.

But the chimerical bird brought him no more luck than it had brought companionship. Clarence—Finch, as he is now—was like that gloomy little man in the funny papers with his own personal rain cloud: misfortune dogged him everywhere, he couldn't win for losing, he was wedded to calamity. Any time he ventured out on the streets of Needmore, keeping a wary eye on the sidewalk, a pigeon was sure to fly over and dump its sodden ballast on his hat, or some old lady to lean out an upstairs window and shake her dust mop over him. Or if, instead, he watched the sky, his foot was just as sure to find a steaming coil of Delano's unsavory business on the pavement, or he would fall off the curb, or a car would come along and splash muddy water on him.

Even aside from the twice-daily horror of the school bus, Finch's life seemed to him an endless round of abominations and persecutions, ill usage and adversity, gall and wormwood, wormwood and gall. The door of his room upstairs wouldn't stay closed, and Pismire kept sneaking in to use his bed for a cat box; and so frequent were the "little accidents" in Claude's noisome pissery—which, unhappily for Finch, doubled as his own bathroom, the only one he had—that he'd begun to suspect Claude's clientele of getting sick in there on purpose, to torment him; and he knew for a fact that they were chewing way more tobacco than they used to, just to keep the spittoons overflowing all the time; and on Saturday afternoons they shot a lot more pool than . . . than decent people ought to shoot, trying to run him ragged racking balls for them and make him have a heart attack, because . . . well, because they wouldn't believe there was anything wrong with him.

Eventually there appeared, taped to the Billiards' back-bar mirror, one of those cartoon postcards depicting a disconsolate-looking little fellow sitting shoulder-deep in a toilet bowl, puling, "GOO'BYE, CROOL WORLD!" with his upraised hand upon the lever, ready to flush himself away. Next to the drawing, the anonymous party who'd posted it had penciled in the name "Finch," to make sure no one would miss his point. The handwriting, Finch could not have failed to note, was unmistakably that of his affectionate half-brother.

When school let out for the summer, Finch hardly noticed. He didn't have to drive his bus by day, of course, but in his dreams the river road unreeled endlessly before him, all those tortured, twisting miles still undriven and the roiling muddy waters waiting far below. Before he knew it, he was back at the wheel again, and young Clabber, fatter, meaner, and uglier than ever, was walloping him convivially on the back of the head to greet him on the occasion of the opening of the new school year. Finch grimaced silently and thought of the old story Maudie used to read him about the Pied Piper, who had led the children into the sea.

And so the weeks and months rolled on, and America fought its war in places Burdock County never heard of, and now and then word came back that a son of Burdock had fallen somewhere, hurt or dead. Eventually, local patriots installed in the courthouse yard a billboard-sized Burdock County Servicemen's Honor Roll, with gold stars for the slain, red stars for the wounded, blue stars for the missing and the captured. Among the luckless heroes were several in whose company Finch had made the trip to Mount Ararat that dreadful day—including the one who'd pantsed him (red star, in the Philippines), the one who'd peed in his hat (red star, at Guadalcanal), and the one who'd thrown it out the window (gold star, felled by a mortar at Anzio). Finch was unable to suppress the apprehension that a terrible kind of justice might be at work here, yet he took no satisfaction from it—for he was himself no stranger to loss and suffering, and nowadays it sometimes seemed to him that grief was everywhere, as omnipresent as a long spell of bad weather.

One of Finch's lesser sorrows during those dark days was the slow but inexorable dismantling and befoulment of the homeplace at the hands of the irrepressibly squalid Skirvins, under the indulgent eye of Claude, their landlord, who was actually rather enjoying the process, this little bonus contribution to his brother's misery. With every passing day, Finch noted to his disheartenment, there seemed to be more Skirvins on the place, and more Skirvin residue. There were Skirvins everywhere, a dozen or more at any given moment in the house where Finch had lately dwelt in solitary splendor: Waldo and his wife Goldie and their five children and Goldie's brother Chump Slackert and Chump's wife Myrtle and their two children and a parade of old aunties and uncles and half-wit cousins wandering back and forth from the Burdock County poorhouse a few miles down the road, where all Skirvins and Slackerts seemed, eventually, to end up.

The weeds took Maudie's flower bed like a panzer unit, and the front yard was soon ankle-deep in tin cans, broken bottles, automobile parts, potato peelings, tobacco chaws, dog droppings, and other Skirvin spoor that had just as well remain undescribed. The picket fence went up the chimney their first winter on the place; the front porch followed, then the shutters, then the barn doors, then the privy door—for if there had been a Skirvin lexicon, the word *modesty* would not have been included. They would've torn the stripping room off the barn and burned that too, except that Waldo's old one-armed daddy was living in it; they would, indeed, have burned the barn itself, but for their landlord's Sunday afternoon crapshoot and cockfight socials, on which that enterprising gent was making money by the fistful.

"If M-Mommy seen the way them Skir-kir-kirvins has done her flowers," Finch ventured to complain at last, "she would turn over in her gr-gr-gr- . . ."

"Let 'er roll, baby brother, let 'er roll!" cheerfully rejoined the rightful scion of the House of Craycraft. "She ain't got nothing else to do, has she?"

In early 1944, a blue star appeared beside the name of Pfc. Claude Elrod Craycraft; the valiant Buster had been taken in northern Italy, doubtless after a terrific struggle, and was to sit out the remainder of the war in a German POW camp, where—according to a report that filtered back from a Burdock County lad who was imprisoned in the same camp—he attained great celebrity among his fellow prisoners for snitching on them to their captors at every opportunity.

Meanwhile, back on the home front, the fair Iota kept her knight-errant's memory alive by continuing annually to produce fat, mean little uglies just as though he weren't gone, thanks to the good offices of Buster's old pal Chick Greevey, who'd had to miss the war after inadvertently lopping off his trigger finger with a meat cleaver the day before his scheduled induction into the army and who had subsequently taken on the servicing of Iota as an alternative patriotic duty.

———

In the dreary depths of March in 1945, Finch came upon an ad in the local weekly announcing that a certain P. Cosmo Rexroat, Doctor of Natural Theosophy, Chiropractic Science, and Colonic Irrigation, distinguished graduate of the Universidad del Medico Diagnostico of Nuevo Laredo, Mexico, would be holding private consultations for a limited time only at the Rexroat Mobile Diagnostic Clinic in the city of Limestone, diagnosing and treating ailments of the heart, lungs, liver, kidneys, stomach, spine, joints, digestive system, nervous system, and feet, with female complaints a specialty, not to say a calling. The ad featured—but did not depict—an apparatus of the doctor's own invention, called the Electro Magno-Static Diagnosis Machine, a modern scientific miracle that was said to possess the capability of reading the patient's inner workings like a road map, instantly directing the attending physician to the trouble spot without the subject's experiencing the slightest pain or discomfort whatsoever. Cash payments only, no appointments necessary.

Now here was a doctor a man could depend on and have a little faith in. Not one of your stick-in-the-mud backwoods hick country quacks, neither, but a fellow with some get-up-and-go about him, which had went abroad and studied up on all the latest progressive modernistic scientific advances. Early the next day, right after his morning bus run, Finch fired up the Plymouth and hied himself to Limestone.

The Rexroat Mobile Diagnostic Clinic occupied a beat-up old house trailer parked in a weedy vacant lot beside a beer joint called Charlie's Dream Bar, and the Electro-Magno-Static Diagnosis Machine turned out to be a more or less exact replica of that grim fixture known in gangster movies as the Hot Seat, next to which was a panel mounted with a bewildering array of wires, switches, knobs, lights, bells, vacuum tubes, transformers, and other electro-magno-static what-have-you, and one large round dial labeled around its perimeter with the terms "Cancer," "Gallstones," "Heart Disease," "Brain Tumor," "Tuberculosis," and all the other ills with which the sicklings might suppose themselves afflicted.

Dr. Rexroat's nurse and trusted laboratory assistant, a gruff, barrel-chested, oakum-haired woman of rugged aspect and raw demeanor, strapped and clamped the terrified Finch into this disconcerting article of furniture ("Christ on a crutch, hon," she muttered, as to an errant child, "stop that goddamn squirmin', will ya!"), and then, with her patient securely pinioned in the chair, said she'd just slip next door to the Dream Bar to fetch the doctor.

She returned several long moments later with the great diagnostician firmly in tow, a dirty little gray gent whose entrance immediately added the heady bouquet of bay rum and blended whiskey to the already somewhat close and fulsome atmosphere inside the trailer. The doctor boozily inquired of Finch just what he thought his trouble might be, then made "a few minor adjustments" behind the instrument panel, and without further ceremony, threw the switch. Bells clanged, lights flashed, a slight shock coursed through Finch's body, and the red pointer on the big dial leaped from its post and flew like love's own arrow straight to the "D" in "Heart Disease."

"It *did*!" as Finch told it later in the Billiards, so excited that for the first time in his life (though not the last, as we have seen), he almost forgot to stammer. "And that doctor told me, Mr. Fronk, he says, it is a act of God you're still a-living, for you got as bad a case of 'c-cute heart disease as ever I treated! And he said I was to come back on Friday and let him irritate my c-colon for me! And he never charged me but twenty dollars, and for two dollars extry he throwed in this free book!"

The book was a slim volume entitled *Prayers for My Good Health*, by the Very Reverend P. Cosmo Rexroat. Finch pored over it, and doted on it, and pronounced the reverend doctor the savior of his life and soul.

The Billiards crowd was impressed; they'd never known a certified act of God before—or, at any rate, they hadn't known they knew one. Claude scoffed at first, of course, but when Finch showed him Dr. Rexroat's chapter entitled "A Prayer for My Enlarged Liver"—a condition with which Claude was intimately acquainted, it being an occupational hazard of his profession—and Claude observed that the doctor prescribed colonic irrigation and an occasional petition to the Almighty but didn't say a word about not drinking fifteen or twenty bottles of beer every day, even he decided there might be something to it. And so, for a couple of days, Finch's credibility was at an all-time high.

The Friday of Finch's appointment happened to be Good Friday, and school let out at noon. By early afternoon he was on the road to Limestone, thinking as he drove that he'd probably feel so invigorated by his treatment that he might just have to hang around town till evening and pay a little call on Mrs. Mooney.

Alas, it was not to be. When Finch arrived at the site of the Rexroat Mobile Diagnostic Clinic, there was in the vacant lot only vacancy, and weeds, and the three cinder blocks that had served as the clinic's doorstep. Finch went next door to the Dream Bar to find out what had happened, and Charlie, the proprietor, told him they'd left town in the dead of night after the wife of the mayor of Limestone had brought her female troubles to the doctor and had been singed bald-headed by a crossed wire in the Electro-Magno-Static Diagnosis Machine.

"And y'know," said Charlie, "I'm gonna miss that little old bastard, too. He was smart as a tack, the way he would set around in here and talk in them big words and tell you the sayings of Shakespeare and whatnot. He kinda dressed the place up, like, and I enjoyed him, know what I mean? Last time he was here, he run up a pretty good tab, and then he says, 'Charles, my boy'—he would always call me Charles— 'Charles, I fear I am suffering from a temporary embarrassment of funds,' or some bull like that, and says would I perhaps accept a copy of this book which he had wrote hisself? Well, I seen he had me, because I liked the old rip, and wouldn't've called the law on him under no circumstances. So I says, 'Reverent, I will, by god. But I want you to autograft it personal for me.' And he done that, and here"— Charlie took down a copy of *Prayers for My Good Health* from the back-bar shelf and opened it to the flyleaf and passed it over the bar to Finch—"is what he put down in it. I can't make heads nor tails out of it myself, but I'm real proud to have it, just the same."

"Every man" (Finch read, steeped to the lips in misery) "should have a motto, Charles, and I take mine from the Immortal Bard. To wit:

> *Diseases desperate grown,*
> *By desperate appliance are relieved,*
> *Or not at all.*

"Warmest personal regards, P. Cosmo Rexroat, B.S., M.S., Ph.D."

———

Then at last the war was over, and by ones and twos the boys—now men—came straggling home, some with medals on their chests, a few with an empty sleeve or a prosthetic leg, one with wild eyes and ruined nerves and a metal plate in his head. Then too, of course, there were those who did not come at all, except in the form of little packets containing dog tags and personal effects. Some of the returnees went back to their jobs or their trades or the family farm as if they'd never left, some joined the 52-20 club—twenty dollars a week in government "readjustment" money for fifty-two weeks—

and ran around the county like madmen for a year, drinking and carousing, some took the GI Bill and went to college and, for all practical Burdock County purposes, disappeared from the face of the earth forever. All of them, it seems safe to say, had seen more than country boys were ever meant to see, and Burdock County would never look quite the same to them again.

For a time, Finch allowed himself to hope that the end of the war would bring about some small easing of his own woes. Buster would be wanting his old bus route back, he reasoned, so Claude would just have to find Finch something else to do. Maybe, if they could somehow dislodge the Skirvins, he could even go back to the farm, or what was left of it, and learn to milk this time, and to garden a little, and to clean his own fish—his stomach was stronger now, thanks to the regular testing it had been put to in the pissery—and manage to keep himself, for whatever little dab of time was left to him.

But when Chick Greevey heard that Buster was on his way home, he took off like a scalded dog for parts unknown (Buster wasn't much of a threat, but then it didn't require much of a threat to send Chick Greevey scurrying), leaving the dead wagon without a driver—a line of work that was more to Buster's liking than the school bus had been, since the dead animals weren't on any particular schedule and didn't oblige a troop to muster his ass outta the rack at oh-five-hunnert hours (Buster hadn't been much of a soldier either, but he came home speaking Military as though it were his native tongue) to drive them here and there around the goddamn countryside, and also your dead animals would lay still and not worry the ass off a troop which was trying his level goddamn best to get them to school on time, where they could get some education and improve their goddamn selfs a little bit.

Buster scarcely deigned to notice that whereas he'd left home the father of three with a fourth on the way, he returned less than four years later the father of six with a seventh on the way. Iota's genes having held dominion over both his and Chick's, all the children looked just alike anyhow —so what the hell, Buster said philosophically, Iota wasn't no Betsy Grable, but after a troop's ass has set nineteen goddamn months in a goddamn Noxie hellhole, nookie's nookie, ain't it?

———

One sultry August afternoon in 1947, not many days after his contretemps with the amorous Delano, Finch sat on an iron bench in the courthouse yard through a sudden, violent thunderstorm, drenched and trembling, trusting the iron to draw the lightning down. When neither physics nor metaphysics would oblige him he lifted his hands to the angry, fulminating heavens, silently imploring *Why me, Lord? Why m-me?*—and was answered on the instant by a prodigious bolt of lightning that split the top out of a courthouse elm not twenty yards away and then, as Finch scurried belatedly for cover, by a peal of thunder as tremendous as God's colossal rejoinder in the old joke: "BECAUSE . . . YOU . . . PISS . . . ME . . . OFF!"

His purpose in life, Finch saw now all too clearly, was to provide, by his sufferings, for the amusement and diversion of his fellowman. By little and little, Finch's dread of his departure from this mortal coil had almost entirely given way to a deep, inchoate longing to begin the journey, a longing not so much to die as merely to be . . . elsewhere, to be *taken*, to join those shadowy legions known as The Departed.

But God's mercy is yet another commodity upon which we ought never to presume. How could Finch, in the toils of that unhappiest of summers, have dreamed that before the coming school year was as much as two weeks old, love would arrive like a late-blooming flower in the barren door-yard of his life and bring him a purer joy than any he had ever known?

For this was to be no profane, two-dollar love, no Mrs. Mooney kind of love; this was an exalted, even a godly love, the love of a father for a son, in whom he is privileged to recognize both himself and some faint intimation of a glory far beyond himself. Miraculously, the son that was born to Finch in the fall of 1947 was already nine years old. All the more remarkable, he was neither a Fronk nor yet even a Craycraft, but . . . a Skirvin!

———

Of Goldie Skirvin's five living babies, Brownie had been the last and certainly the least, weighing in as he did at four and a half pounds, a month early. A few days after his arrival, when the county health officer showed up to certify the birth, Goldie still hadn't thought of—indeed she hadn't even thought *about*—a name for the little sojourner, because she'd hardly dared to hope that he'd be with her long enough to need it. She'd lose this one, she warned herself, the way she'd lost the three otherns that come puny.

So when the health officer went to fill out the birth certificate, she'd snapped, "Names is gettin' skeerce these days, y'know!" to put him off for a minute, so she could think.

But then the only thing that came into her mind was the name of a little old dog she'd had one time, a mangy little old feist that wasn't no account for nothing, but had bit Waldo once when he was drunk and needed biting, and had finally went and got itself run over by the mailman and caused her to cry over it when she pitched its little body in the sinkhole, because it had the saddest, sweetest big brown eyes that had looked right back at a person even from the bottom of the sinkhole, just exactly the way this little old baby looked up at you from down there in the warsh basket where it was a-laying. So she named it Brownie, after the dog, on account of sentimental reasons.

Well, like Finch before him, Brownie had lived but he hadn't thrived; now, in his ninth year, he was a head shorter than the next tallest of his third-grade classmates, and as thin as a shitepoke, with rickety legs and bad teeth and, beneath the dirt, an inauspicious pallor. Yet his tiny, doll-like features, framed by tangled sorrel curls and graced by his namesake's big brown limpid eyes, were not without a certain shy, fragile beauty—which automatically made him the mortal enemy of Clawvern Craycraft, Buster's boy, arguably the most ill-favored of Iota's unlovely spawn.

Like his older brother and his several winsome sisters, Clawvern was distinguished by an ovoid anatomy, green-rinded teeth, a disagreeable nature, and the presence at all times of one or the other forefinger in one or the other nostril. All in all, he was as loathsome a dirty necked, knot-headed, misbuttoned, snot-besotted, mossy-toothed, eczema-ridden little mouth-breathing article of juvenile degeneracy as ever graced the halls of Burdock County Elementary. His scholarship also distinguished him; though he was going on thirteen, he'd only made it to the fourth grade so far—incontrovertible evidence, in Clawvern's view, of the failings of the Burdock County educational establishment.

So, to balance the scales, Clawvern had lately taken upon himself the education and forming into manhood of young Brownie Skirvin, to which purpose—"to make him *smart!*" Clawvern guffawed—he cuffed and pinched and tweaked and pummeled the little fellow tirelessly; he sat behind him on the bus and pulled his hair and flipped his ears; he entertained him with hotfoots and Dutch rubs or thumped his Adam's apple as though it were a cantaloupe. To teach him family values and the virtues of good breeding, he regularly made a point of reminding Brownie that his father was a souse, his mother was a scagmaw, his brothers were burglars, and his sisters were punchboards.

One day, noting that Brownie looked a little peaked, Clawvern prescribed one of his own personal slightly used tobacco chaws and saw to it that Brownie worked the delicacy until he'd derived maximum nourishment from it, as evidenced by his turning green and throwing up in the aisle. That's how you worm a pup (Clawvern assured him, all noblesse oblige), and you worm a Skirvin the same damn way.

And for all these services and considerations, the only return Clawvern exacted was the five cents Goldie somehow managed to scrounge together every day for Brownie's lunch, which would have been—if he were ever allowed to eat it—a nickel's worth of cheese and crackers at the grocery store across the street from the school yard. Instead, Claw-

vern now topped off his own light lunch—two baloney sandwiches and a Pepsi—with a Milky Way, courtesy of the
humbler classes.

And should Brownie even think of protesting these very
pleasant arrangements, Clawvern would be obliged, he
warned, to report the insubordination to his venerable
grandparent, who'd promptly send Waldo and Goldie and
Brownie and Chump and Myrtle and Popaw and them
a-hoofing it down the road to the poorhouse, where they be-
longed.

The end result of Clawvern's attentions, Finch had
noted in his rearview, was that the smaller boy regularly left
the bus with tears welling in those great brown eyes. But although Finch certainly recognized and felt for him as a fellow sufferer, he had plenty of troubles of his own, and at first
it just didn't occur to him that he and Brownie had all that
much in common.

In his own childhood, desolate though it was, Finch
hadn't really been tormented by his schoolmates; in fact,
they'd usually treated him with the most gingerly respect, because big old Ott, in his thick-tongued, menacing way, had
put out the word that if anybody teased the boy and caused
him to have a heart attack, he'd have *der hundsfott* charged
with murder and sent to the electric chair. So they had all
pussyfooted around little Clarence as if the wrong word
might blow him to the winds; his weakness, his very vulnera-
bility had been his armor. But poor Brownie had no defenses
at all—and Finch sure couldn't see himself providing any,
should it ever come to that.

His and Brownie's similitude was not made manifest for
Finch until the day, when that school year was less than two

weeks old, that Brownie's third-grade teacher, Miss Vermillion, passing among her scholars while they were assiduously at their studies, happened to glance down as she passed Brownie's desk and saw, to her horror, that his tousled curls were fairly hopping with . . . well, call them cooties, crumbs, wig rats, shag bunnies, galloping dandruff, or even, as the poet had it, "crawlin' ferlies." In a word, lice.

Miss Vermillion threw up her hands and gasped, "Chinches!" (that having been the popular designation for the species during her own girlhood), and thereby instantly apprized the entire English-speaking world—at least so far as Brownie understood its boundaries—of the wildlife that was just then so enjoying his hospitality.

On the bus that afternoon, Brownie's sympathizers outdid themselves in their zeal. No wonder he had fleas, they said, named for a dog the way he was. But they had plans for his immediate improvement.

"Let's shave off that damn bug rug for 'im!" Clayton Craycraft urged, brandishing his pocketknife.

"Nah," amended Harry Tom Powers, at fifteen a fixture for the past three years in the fifth grade, where he'd acquired so much learning that it threatened to become a burden to him. "Let's shave off *half* of it, see, and set fire to the other half! And when them graybacks runs out into the open, we'll stab 'em with an ice pick!"

Finch, eyeing the rearview mirror as though it were a little window on his memory, had the distinct feeling he'd seen all this before.

Now Clawvern labored to his feet, a squat, lumpish ogre waddling into the aisle. "I got a good ideal!" he squealed, unplugging his forefinger from his nose to make a grab for

Brownie's cap. "Let's pee in his hat and throw it out the winder!"

Now you know! piped the tiny muse on Finch's shoulder. *Now you know, now you know!*

And that's when Finch slammed on the brakes and sent Clawvern tumbling ass over teacups up the aisle, breaking his left arm in two places.

"I thought I seen a c-c-cat," Finch explained that evening in the poolroom to the fuming Buster, who had just plunked down forty-seven dollars to have Clawvern's arm set. "It run right ac-c-c-cross the r-r-r-..."

Clawvern, tearstained and sniveling at his father's side, adorned now from his shoulder to his wrist by nine pounds of plaster, declared that *he* never seen no shitten cat—and kicked his uncle smartly in the shin for emphasis.

"Next time," Buster snarled through clenched teeth, as he dragged Clawvern off by his uninjured limb, "break the goddamn *cat's* arm, will ya!"

Finch was glad Clawvern had kicked him, because the pain in his ankle put a damper on his happiness and kept him from laughing at them right out loud.

Things are not always as they seem, and so it was with Goldie Skirvin, who for all her failings in the areas of personal hygiene and household sanitation—and they were monumental, the stuff of local legend—was, within the narrow limits of her power, a good and certainly a loving mother. Thus it was that every morning before bus time for the next several weeks, she spent half an hour combing coal oil through Brownie's curls, a remedy that had the doubly salutary effects of killing his cooties while simultaneously keeping his other persecutors at a respectful distance.

Not that Brownie was the first to reap the benefits of Goldie's nurturing. Hadn't she about brained Waldo with the frying pan that time he tried to whip Irmadene for getting herself in a family way by some of them Toomes County scallywags? And hadn't she took a whole carton of cigarettes every week of the world to Ronnie and Donnie, her two oldest boys, when they was in jail for breaking into Pincherd's feed store, summer before last? And didn't Bernice, her oldest girl, that was doing real good working in the buckle factory up in Hamilton, Ohio, send her the sweetest Mother's Day card last year and write "SWAK," for "Sealed With A Kiss," on the outside of the envelope? Goldie had even set up half the night giving a sugar-tit to that sorry Myrtle's little baby Elmo when it was colicky the other week, while Chump and Myrtle, the sorry things, was up there in the bed a-wallering to where they rattled the lid on the chamber pot. And if she did have to say so her own self, she took a whole lot better care than *he* did of Waldo's poor old one-armed daddy, Popaw Skirvin, which wasn't no baby she would admit but which was worse than one, the way he messed hisself so bad they'd had to move him out of the house into the stripping room.

But it was for little Brownie that Goldie reserved the roomiest corner of her capacious heart. Because he was so tiny and delicate—and maybe just because she'd so loved holding him, such a baby doll he was—she'd kept him on the breast till he was nearly three, all night long night after night till he'd sucked her dry as a shucky poppet, him lying there in her lap gazing up at her so solemn and grave with that brown unwavering study, as though he saw something deep inside her, something no eyes but his had ever seen. I'm old and ugly and plumb wore out, she used to tell herself sometimes, and this pretty little thing is the only one in all the world, the only one in all my life, that ever really knowed me.

So she loved Brownie best of all, and when that nice young Mr. Fronk came to the door early on a September Saturday and asked her could he take the boy f-f-fishing, she never thought a thing about it, seeing as how (she said later) he looked to her like the harmlessest thing that ever was, standing there on the front step with his little hat in his hands, just a-stuttering and a-twitching. Which all goes to show a person, don't it, that you can't depend on nothing in this day and age.

Finch came almost every Saturday after that. He and the boy would go off down to the river with their fishing poles on their shoulders, carrying the minnow bucket between them, Finch with a little breakfast of baloney sandwiches or Moon Pies or cheese and crackers for them in his pocket, and they'd be gone till up around noon, when Goldie would see them working their way slowly back up the hill through the warm late-summer sunshine, stopping under every shade tree so Finch could rest his heart.

And when they'd got close enough to see Goldie standing in the doorway of the house, watching them, they'd stop and wave, and whichever one was carrying the stringer of fish would hold it up so she could see that they'd caught some, and she'd wave back and then go to the stove and put on a frying pan of lard, to have the grease hot when they got there. She liked her fish rolled in cornmeal, and Finch said that suited him just f-f-fine (though he scarcely ever actually ate any, because, to tell the truth, his stomach still hadn't strengthened to the point that it could handle the state of Goldie's kitchen), so that was how she fixed them.

It being Saturday, Chump and Waldo would've already gone to town, thank the Lord, to get drunk, but Myrtle would always say, Well, yes, she guessed she would *try* a little taste of fish, although she did *perfer* her fish rolled in *flahr* and fried in *bacon* grease—and then she would set right there and eat three or four pieces like they was going out of style.

Then Goldie would have to fry up some for Myrtle's little twins Stella Mae and Mae Stella (about the only thing Goldie and Myrtle agreed on was that names *was* getting awful skeerce nowadays), and the twins would slip bites to Baby Elmo (which they wasn't supposed to do, because Elmo was still on the bottle, and milk and fish is poison, y'know, when you mix them), and Goldie's second girl Irmadene sometimes come over from Toomes County with her bosoms all pooched out of the top of her dress like half of Burdock County—half the men, anyhow—hadn't done seen more of them already than they had any business seeing. And old Aunt Nepp Slackert and her idjit boy Cousin Harold was liable to show up from down at the poorhouse in time for a little snack of fish, and Goldie would always send Brownie out to the stripping room with a piece or two for Popaw, along with a dipperful of cistern water in case he was to get a bone in his old throat.

So they would all have quite a good feast, and Goldie did love the way her little boy's eyes would shine so big and bright when, between mouthfuls of fish, he would tell his new friend Mr. Fronk about his pet black gamecock Joe

Louis (whose fate, time would shortly prove, was that he'd soon be slashed to chicken salad in one of Claude's Sunday afternoon bird-watchers' convocations), or about the rusty old red wagon he'd found under the porch when they tore it off for firewood (Finch's eyes misted over at that; he was remembering Ott and Maudie and a Christmas of long ago), or about how he was teaching Cousin Harold (who was thirty-two years old but, as even Aunt Nepp admitted, "kinely back'ard") to tie his own shoelaces.

And Goldie noticed, as a mother would, that this nice Mr. Fronk fairly beamed whenever he looked upon her boy, and that he always had some little trinket for him in his pocket, a candy cane or a yo-yo or a water pistol or a pencil box, and that sometimes when he reached out to pat the boy on the cheek, his hand would tremble like a leaf. She wondered a little at all this, but at last—because she cared so deeply for the boy herself, and also, perhaps, because she enjoyed a good fish dinner now and then as much as anybody—she listened to the vibrant, thrumming chords of the mothersong within her and concluded—quite correctly, as it happens—that Finch loved her boy for the son he'd never have and that there wasn't no harm in him whatsoever, not in no way, shape, or form.

Which all goes to show a person, don't it now?

———

Meanwhile, on Finch's school bus things had taken, remarkably, a turn for the better. For thanks to one of those sweet little ironies by which Providence reminds us that there is some justice after all, the more vehemently Clawvern Craycraft insisted that Finch's c-c-cat had been a fiction, that there had been no c-c-cat at all, and that Finch had slammed on his brakes for the specific purpose of breaking Clawvern's arm, the higher Finch's stock rose among his passengers and the more precipitously Clawvern's plummeted. Believing Clawvern, even the surliest of his fellows revised in an upwardly direction their low opinion of their driver: any grown man, their instincts told them, who would deliberately set out to break a twelve-year-old boy's arm with a school bus was not to be taken lightly.

And, Harry Tom Powers warned, if Clawvern didn't hush his goddamn pissing and moaning about that goddamn cat, Harry Tom would personally be forced to break Clawvern's other arm for him, and then the little dipshit would have to pick his goddamn nose with his goddamn feet.

In the face of these (and many similar) civilities, Clawvern repaired, more or less permanently, to the furthermost corner of his seat to sulk and to carry on his exploratory nasal probings *in camera*, glaring at the back of Finch's head as if he hoped his very eyebeams might knock that inconsequential article off his uncle's shoulders.

Now for the first time ever, Finch found himself looking forward to the daily bus runs. To his inexpressible delight, Brownie had seemed to understand right away that he had a new friend and protector. Reeking of coal oil—for all that mattered to the doting Finch—he began the very morning after Clawvern's mishap to take the seat on the bus directly behind the driver's seat—in the rearview, his grave little face appeared to be just at Finch's shoulder, as though the wee fabled bird itself had come at last—and from that day forward the seat was his alone.

By the return trip that afternoon, the two of them were

shyly passing the time of day as they rode along, and by the following afternoon, a Friday, Finch, his heartbeat quickening almost alarmingly, heard himself inquire whether Brownie might like to do a little f-fishing one of these days. Yessirree, said the boy, he sure would, and Finch said, Well, how about t-tomorrow? And so they embarked together upon the happiest season of their lives.

For the rest of his days, Finch lived for Saturday mornings. All week long, on the school bus, he and the boy planned their next outing, earnestly considering—and reconsidering, and reconsidering—which holes they'd fish this week, what bait they'd use, what kind of snacks they'd take along, how many fish they intended to catch. On Friday night, Finch could hardly close his eyes, and on many a Saturday morn he spent the last hour before dawn sitting in the car a hundred yards up the road from the homeplace, with the headlights off and the motor running, while he eagerly scanned the eastern horizon for the first pale blessed hint of daylight, so that not a single minute of the precious morning would be wasted.

Intuitively, Finch understood that the less Claude knew about his new affection, the better would be its chances to grow and thrive and prosper. So as best he could, he kept his happiness out of harm's way, slipping out of the poolroom early each Saturday morning before Claude came in to open up and making sure he was back in time to rack balls and tend his spittoons for the Saturday afternoon crowd.

Finch tried to steer clear of Waldo Skirvin, too. Not that, ordinarily, Waldo would've cared—or even noticed —that someone had performed some small kindness for his child. But in return for a roof over his head and a sufficiency of intoxicants to keep him in a more or less continual state of oblivion, Waldo was Claude's bondsman and devoted minion, and if, in some soggy recess of his mind, he were to stumble across the notion that there was something going on that his indulgent proprietor would want to know about, or any little enormity he could perpetrate that might ingratiate him with that eminence, he would not scruple to discharge the office.

———————

Thus did that glorious autumn slip away and the golden Saturdays go tumbling by. And sometimes it seemed to Finch, sitting there on the Yonder's banks with the boy chattering gladsomely beside him while their bobbers danced in the current among the drifting autumn leaves, sometimes it seemed to him that he'd lived his whole life for just these moments, that all his fear and loneliness and suffering were but a long, uneasy dream, and that his present happiness was the only reality that there had ever been in all the everlasting history of the world.

Sundays—cockfight day, that fall—were the longest day of Finch's week, because on Sunday both Claude and Waldo hung around the barn at the homeplace all day long, and there was no chance at all that he and the boy could be together.

Waldo was the trainer and cornerman for Claude's stable of feathered warriors, which for all their unappeasable bellicosity when they were securely snaffled at a safe distance from one another in the front yard of the homeplace, nonetheless sometimes exhibited a singular meekness of spirit in actual combat situations. (The Sunday that poor Joe Louis went into the tank, Brownie told Finch, Brownie had snuck up to the barn just in time to see his august parent scoop up the limp and bloodied bird and take its beak between his lips and seem to blow it up like a rooster-shaped balloon, to the robust cheers of a crowd of men clutching bouquets of greenbacks in their fists—all to no avail, for moments later Joe Louis's opponent deflated him again, this time for good and all.) Rumor had it that their want of pluck owed something to Waldo's practice of surreptitiously introducing, suppository style, certain soporifics, muscle relaxants, and deadweights—once, it was said, a four-ounce plumb bob—into the hindmost apertures of his paladins. And indeed, it must be owned that Claude, who, ever the considerate host, covered the little wagers by means of which the other sporting gentlemen demonstrated their support of these wholesome athletic endeavors, did seem to reveal, now and then, a remarkable clairvoyance as to their outcome, and profited accordingly.

But as busy as Claude was on Sundays with his social responsibilities, Finch knew from long experience that his half-brother's muddy yellow eye never missed a trick; and even Waldo, whose Sunday duties obliged him to maintain at least a minimal level of sobriety, would be a good deal sharper than was ordinarily his habit.

One restless Sabbath, nonetheless, Finch did allow himself to go out for a little Sunday drive, in the course of which he just sort of happened inadvertently to mosey past the homeplace, where it was his amazing happiness to catch sight of Brownie sitting on the front step, playing with the yo-yo Finch had brought him the day before. Finch tooted the horn discreetly as he passed; they waved to one another, and Finch went home to his little room, which was scarcely large enough to contain the memory of that brief joy.

Brownie wasn't alone, though, in marking Finch's passage before the homeplace that afternoon. Up in the barn lot behind the house, Claude Craycraft himself had just stepped outside, momentarily alone with his always interesting thoughts, to take a meditative leak among the parked cars and pickup trucks of his guests. He too noted the Plymouth's passing, the faint tooting of the horn, the furtive wave.

Now who's he honkin' at? Claude mused, contemplatively hosing the dust off the hubcap of somebody's spanking new '47 Chevy. It occurred to him that Finch had maybe taken a shine to Goldie Skirvin or Myrtle Slackert, but he dismissed the thought as quickly as it came when, in the little adding machine that served him for a mind, he totaled up those ladies' personal attractions and found that—unless you counted Goldie's all too natural perfume, or the single gold tooth that prominently graced Myrtle's otherwise almost toothless smile—the sum came to absolute dead zero. Nah, Claude reckoned, buttoning up; the high and mighty little shit-ass likely thinks he's way too good for Myrtle and Goldie.

"You keep a eye on him," Claude instructed Buster, later that day. "We don't want some little shit-ass of a Fronk to disgrace the name of Craycraft."

———

Came a cold, rainy Saturday morning in November and, the fishing being less than promising, Finch put the boy in the Plymouth and took him to the Poll Parrot shoe store in Limestone and bought him a new pair of high-tops with heel and toe taps, and then to Western Auto and bought him a fishknife with a special hook-remover blade, and then to the barbershop—Goldie's coal oil treatments having finally dislodged the colony of tiny squatters from his scalp—for the first store-bought haircut of his life, and then to the B & M Grill for two chili dogs and a Dr. Pepper.

Afterward, as they made their way back to the car along Limestone's rain-wet sidewalks, Brownie suddenly paused and tucked his little hand into Finch's only slightly larger one and piped, "Know what, Mr. Fuffronk?"—that being his innocent transliteration of the way Finch himself pronounced his name—"Them was the best chili dogs that ever I et!" They walked on, hand in hand, the new shoes ticktocking along like a dollar watch, Finch's heart filled near to bursting with paternal pride.

And so intent were they upon each other—or, if you will, so powerful was the heady reek of Florida Water rising from Brownie's slick new haircut—that as they crossed the street with the traffic light at the corner of Main and Bank, they neither saw nor even caught a whiff of Buster Craycraft's dead wagon, though they passed beneath its very snout while it sat, throbbing and muttering, waiting for the light to change.

But Buster, at the wheel, saw *them*, you may be sure, and when he did he turned to his passenger—none other than Clawvern of the broken wing, who'd come to town with Buster that day to have his cast removed—and shook his head, clucked his tongue, curled his lip, seized Clawvern's knee and squeezed it affectionately enough to make him wince, and said, "Holdin' hands, ain't that cute! You keep a eye on that little shit-ass, hon. Daddy *said* he was up to somethin'!"

————

"Holdin' hands, who'd-a thought it!" Claude Craycraft exulted, rubbing his own hands together as gleefully as a sorcerer over a seething cauldron when Buster and Clawvern drew him back by the pissery to report their uncle's latest transgression across the bounds of human decency. "I always knew he was some kinda gizmo! But Lord, boys, ain't it a blessing, there ain't a drop of Craycraft blood in him!"

Still, Claude was a bookmaker, not a gambler; he liked short odds better than long and a sure thing best of all—and he didn't see a sure thing here, not just yet. Patience, that was the trick. Wait till the bird was in the hand, where a man could get a-holt of it by the shorthairs.

Finch, then, remained for the time being blissfully at large, free to perpetrate new outrages on an unsuspecting Christian citizenry. If he felt the crosshairs of official Craycraft scrutiny upon him, well, that was nothing new, and he was undaunted by it.

Indeed, if anything, he even became, in the fullness of his heart, a little bolder. When the coming of early winter drove him and Brownie from the riverbank, Finch, casting about in his mind for something to occupy their Saturday mornings, hit upon the Limestone Opera House, a crumbling, rat-infested old vaudeville theater that now showed triple-feature westerns twenty-four hours a day, a dime a ticket, for the enlightenment of a handful of snoring winos and derelicts who couldn't quite finance a thirty-five-cent bed at the Star Hotel, which was upstairs in the same building. By a few minutes after eight o'clock each Saturday morning, Finch and his little companion would be settled in their second-row seats, gnawing on three-day-old popcorn and cheering the heroics of Johnny Mack Browne or Wild Bill Elliott or Bob Steele or Lash LaRue or, on really good Saturdays, the great Gene, the great Roy.

For Finch, who'd been an old man since the day he was

born, these were the Saturdays he'd been waiting for all his life. During his own boyhood—if you could call it that— Maudie, fearful that the excitement might prove too much for him, had never let him go to the picture show in Needmore, so it was all as new to him as it was to Brownie. If he was Brownie's spiritual father during all his other waking hours, while they were in the Opera House he was just another little boy, pal of his pal, his buddy's buddy. When the lights went down and their looming heroes took their turn upon the screen, Finch and Brownie hunkered low in their seats and leaned toward one another in the dark as small boys—and lovers—will, shoulders touching, heads together, hearts racing side by side to the rhythm of the pounding hooves of Wild Bill's pinto paint.

And that was the tableau on the last Saturday morning before Christmas, when down the darkened aisle sidled a squat little figure who stole like a diminutive gumshoe into the row of seats just behind them and stood for a long moment looking directly down on the oblivious pair, as if he contemplated collaring them on the spot for some nameless indecency or crime. The interloper's aspect was obscure in the flickering shadows, but an observant witness might have noted that his forefinger was firmly implanted in his nose and that when at last he moved along, he left hanging in the stale air the faint dead-wagon fetor of putrescence.

On the afternoon of Christmas Eve, Finch went to the bank and drew twenty dollars out of his little savings account (he'd been putting away ten dollars a month ever since he moved to town—for his funeral, he supposed; not for his old age, certainly), and then he drove to Limestone, where he bought Brownie a Red Ryder model Daisy BB gun at the Western Auto store. While the clerk went off to get a box, Finch took up the little rifle and put it to his shoulder and sighted down the barrel, and imagined he was Wild Bill Elliott in the last Red Ryder movie they had seen and that Brownie was at his side with a feather in his curls, playing Little Beaver. Later, driving home to Needmore with the package on the seat beside him, Finch was all aglow with happiness and pride; you could've followed him through the dusky evening like the star of Bethlehem.

Alas, his happiness was even shorter-lived than usual; it went out like a light when, as he tried to creep unnoticed through the crowded poolroom to the back stairs, his sharp-eyed brother goosed him with a cue stick and hollered, "Whoops!" Finch threw up his hands, and the package slipped from beneath his coat and clattered to the floor.

"Whoa there, Goosey! I believe you dropped the set outta that diamond ring I gave you!" Elbowing Finch aside, Claude bent and picked up the package himself and squinted at the label. "Why, a BB gun, is it! You wasn't planning to shoot yourself, I hope?"

"Oh, n-no!!" Finch said, half apologetically, as though he hated to be such a wet blanket. Beyond Claude, he saw Waldo Skirvin at the bar, mercifully a-snooze, his head pillowed on his arm. "It's j-just a Ch-Christmas p-p-p-p—"

"A Christmas present!" Claude interjected, with a grin that was a hideous, leering mockery of the convivialities of the season. "Bless your heart, it's for that sweet grandboy of mine, that little Clawvern! You just leave that right here with me, baby brother," he went on, tucking the package firmly under his arm, "and I'll be old Santy for you and put it under his tree tonight!"

Horrified, Finch undertook to utter a tiny peep of protest, but Claude said not to thank him, because what were brothers for? He stashed the BB gun out of sight behind the bar; then, herding Finch along before him by means of a couple of discreet pokes in the ribs with the cue stick, he steered him out of earshot of the other players, where he took the liberty of politely reminding him (waggling the cue stick under Finch's nose for emphasis) that even a Skirvin has his pride and wouldn't necessarily be overjoyed when some rich nabob with bad morals came along, throwing his goddamn inheritance around like it wasn't no tomorrow, and tried to give one of the little Skirvins things that was way too fine for him and would spoil him rotten and hurt his daddy's feelings in the bargain, beings as Waldo wasn't in no position to give the boy so much as a hatful of shit his own self, because deep down inside Waldo was as sensitive as . . . as the next man and would sooner see the boy do without.

"And speakin' of Waldo," Claude added as he turned back to his game, "he took a smidge too much Christmas cheer and had one of his little accidents in your pissery. So you got some catchin' up to do, my lad."

"B-Bad m-m-morals?" Finch called bleakly after him, in a voice as faint as a dying breath.

Claude, chalking up, favored him with another fraternal leer. "And a Merry Christmas to *you*, baby brother!" he called back, with vast holiday bonhomie. "Yes, by god, and a Happy New Year, too!"

On New Year's Eve, Waldo Skirvin's proud but sensitive nature required him to heave a pint gin bottle—empty, of course—through the plate-glass window of Hunsicker's

Home Furnishings, enabling him to reach inside and turn on the television set in the window display so that he and Chump could watch midget wrestling. Waldo was rewarded for this unprecedented exhibition of initiative with a forty-five-day expense-paid vacation in the Burdock County jail.

Chump, though he stoutly maintained that all in the world *he* had done was hand Waldo the bottle and urge him to throw it, would be sharing the accommodations for the first thirty days of Waldo's temporary respite from the liquid vortex that was his life.

So for the next several weeks a principal impediment to Finch's happiness would be in cold storage, out of the picture. Yet the development failed to cheer him. Ever since Christmas, Finch had labored under a heavy foreboding, unable to shake the feeling that something ominous and menacing was afoot, stalking him. People were looking at him differently, he was sure, watching him out of the corners of their eyes, talking about him behind his back. Instead of teasing him the way they used to, the Billiards crowd seemed to fall silent whenever he came in, as if teasing were too good for him. Sometimes, when he was sweeping up the poolroom, he would feel their eyes on him, like the weight of an unfriendly hand.

Once, glancing up, he thought he saw—he was *positive* he'd seen—Geezer Wirtschaffner lean toward his neighbor at the bar and, still eyeing Finch in that knowing way, mouth the words *"Bad morals!"* while poor Finch stood there trembling in his shoes, he knew not why.

On the first school day after New Year's, Burdock County awoke beneath a downy five-inch blanket of untracked snow. No school. By the following day, the snow was a foot deep and still falling; no school. That night the temperature dropped below zero, where it was to remain, unprecedented in local memory, for the ensuing thirty-two days, while the Yonder River froze solid for the first time ever. Meanwhile, the snow kept falling until it reached the unheard-of depth of twenty-one inches. No school, no school, no school.

Finch was desolate. Some guardian instinct had advised him to keep his distance from Brownie after Christmas, so the last time they'd been together was the day Clawvern had detected them in unholy congress with Wild Bill Elliott at the Opera House.

Finch missed the boy desperately, but he had consoled himself with the thought that school would soon reopen, and then he'd see him twice a day no matter what. Now, imprisoned in the poolroom by the snow and cold, it seemed to Finch that his whole life had frozen in place, holding him suspended like the fish at the bottom of the Yonder.

———

The weather, having driven Needmore society indoors, straightway set about to drive it stark staring mad with cabin fever. The Billiards crowds grew larger by the day and more restive and surlier—ugly to look at, uglier to deal with. By the end of their second week in captivity, fistfights and scuffles were breaking out among them almost hourly, and billiard balls flew through the air like snowballs; the sawed-off, leaded cue stick that Claude kept behind the bar for a coldcock was regularly employed, as Claude happily rapped out a steady tattoo on the skulls of his irascible clientele.

Cringing and cowering, Finch went about his work, trying desperately to remain below the fray, out of sight and out of mind. You could hardly see daylight through the little black cloud that fulminated above his head.

Out in the countryside, meanwhile, frozen poultry had begun dropping from the roosts like feathered coconuts, and livestock was expiring at an apocalyptic rate, cows freezing upright in the barnyard, hog wallows turning overnight into shallow gravesites as hard as concrete for half-buried pigs as stiff as alabaster statues of themselves. Buster's dead wagon, a heavy rig with dual wheels and a winch for pulling itself out of trouble, had the snowy back roads pretty much to itself. Cruising through town with a truckload of belly-up carcasses, Buster might have been mistaken for a dealer in some macabre line of four-poster beds.

Late one Saturday afternoon in the bitter dregs of January, the winter claimed its first poolroom victim when the aged Delano, having taken a bad cold, relinquished the ghost. Delano's passing was attended by a circle of mourners, most of whom, anticipating the worst, had already got a head start on the wake and were as drunk as fiddlers. As the old dog breathed his last and slipped into a state of dignity that had been resolutely denied him in his lifetime, a ragged hue and cry arose among the survivors to the general effect that Finch was now a widow ... which prompted Buster to advance the theory that Delano had died of a broken heart, upon hearing the rumor that Finch was partial to ... well, Buster would rather not say, due to delicate family considerations.

"I knowed this boy's daddy," Geezer Wirtschaffner reminded them all, waggling that bony forefinger at Finch so emphatically that once again, for the merest fraction of a moment, Finch thought Geezer was on his side. "Knowed him well," Geezer went on. "He had as fine a head of hair as ever I put a scissor to. You ain't half the man he was, sonny boy. It wasn't one ounce of sissy in that old man's body."

Claude, during this interval, had grieved his fill. "Junior," he snapped, "go pitch that dog in the dead wagon." He turned to Finch. "You go to your room, Petunia. I won't be needin' you this evening."

Dejectedly, Finch followed orders, trudging off through a hail of insult and disparagement, knowing full well he'd have to pay some awful price for this unwelcome night off. Upstairs, he flung himself across his little bed and fell, in time, into an uneasy sleep and a dream in which he and Brownie galloped a great white stallion across an endless western plain. He was awakened just after midnight—closing time—by a fearsome pounding on the floor beneath his bed; Claude was downstairs hammering on the ceiling with the butt of a cue stick.

"Hump your ass down here, Daisy Mae!" Claude shouted up the stairwell. "I wanna have a word or three with you!"

Finch found his brother behind the bar at the till, counting his receipts. The poolroom was in its predictably deplorable Saturday night condition—empties everywhere, spittoons overflowing, the floor carpeted with cigarette butts—and Finch knew without even looking that numerous little accidents would have transpired in the pissery.

Claude went right to the point. "I tell you what it is,

bub," he said. "Some way or the other, people around here has got the notion you're up to somethin' with that little Skirvin."

"B-Big brother," Finch pleaded, "you d-don't think I . . ."

"It don't make jack-shit what *I* think. There ain't but two schools of thought you need to worry about, see. One of 'em says you oughta be tarred and feathered, and the othern is holdin' out for corncobs and turpentine."

But, he continued (while Finch clung to the bar and tried not to faint dead away), Claude Craycraft was the kind of hairpin that done his duty as he seen it, so he had just took the bull by the shorthairs and rode out to the homeplace the other day with Buster and told Goldie Skirvin just exactly how the land laid, and him and her agreed that the thing to do was to pack up her and the boy and take them over to Limestone and put them on the Greyhound and send them up to Hamilton, Ohio, to live with Bernice, which Junior done this very afternoon at Claude's own expense—set him back eleven dollars and seventy cents for the bus tickets—and now what Finch was to do was just lay low and keep his nose clean and mind his P's and Q's while Claude undertook to put the quietus on the turpentiners, and maybe by the time Finch was fifty-five or sixty years old (heh heh), all this would've blowed over.

"They've done g-gone?" Finch gulped.

"This very afternoon," Claude said. "But they say the boy has got TB and ain't long for this world anyhow. So you won't be missing much."

"T-t-t-t-tee b-b-b-b-b-b—?"

"Bee," Claude finished for him. "So"—he handed Finch

his mop and bucket—"you better just get started swabbin' out your pissery, Mr. High and Mighty, and leave the dirty work to me."

Finch would've turned to go, but Claude still held the handle of the bucket.

"And lookahere, John D., they tell me you've got money in the bank" (indeed, Claude had known about Finch's little bank account from the very first, and over the years had formed the habit of mentally calculating its growth so that at any given moment he knew its value almost to the penny— and as Finch's next of kin, considered it practically his own), "they tell me you've got a wad of money in the bank, but I'd take it very personal if you was to send a goddamn nickel of it to that poor child, which won't live long enough to spend it anyhow."

Finch nodded mutely, and Claude turned him loose. Bemused, he watched him go, feeling that on the whole, it had been a very satisfying interview.

———

The weather broke on the following Tuesday with a vengeance. A warm southern breeze had swept across the commonwealth in the night, and by midmorning it had brought a steady downpour with it, which continued, more or less unabated, for a solid week. The snow vanished almost overnight, but the ground beneath it was frozen so hard and so deep that it carried off the water like a tin roof; innocent freshets became instant raging torrents, dry branches roaring sluices of destruction. The ice in the Yonder broke up quickly and then formed monumental ice jams that clogged the channel and forced the burgeoning river from its banks. Flash floods abounded, and half the roads in Burdock County were soon under water. School would have to wait.

It was all the same to Finch; he was ready whenever they were. Let it happen.

Deep inside himself, Finch had changed almost as dramatically as the weather. He had peered into the shallows (there were no depths) of the Enemy's very soul and had found nothing there but obdurate, pitiless rancor. He'd never see his boy again; not in this life, he knew that. But with that grievous knowledge came a kind of grace; there being nothing left to live for, he was released at last from the fear of dying and in its stead was gripped by the savage courage of the implacable avenger. He would put his faith in a just and angry god and be ready to play his small part when the time came.

―――――――

When at last the skies had wrung themselves dry and a pale, cheerless winter sun emerged, the fractious creeks crept grudgingly back inside their banks, taking with them as many outhouses and chicken coops as they could get their watery clutches on. One by one, the back roads cleared; on Valentine's Day—exactly forty-one days after that first infamous snowflake fell to earth—the school board announced that as of tomorrow morning, school was back in session.

Chump Slackert, meanwhile, having served his time and been declared a free man, had for the last two weeks been exercising his First Amendment rights by ventilating to all the world his loud assurance that the first thing his brother-in-law Waldo Skirvin planned to do when *he* got out of jail was to tear Finch Fronk a brand-new nether orifice.

On the face of it, this report needn't have troubled Finch all that much; even if Waldo—who'd have his liberty at noon tomorrow—managed to stay sober long enough to carry out Chump's threat, Finch was prepared to suffer and was eager—more than eager—to expire. But his own revenge took precedence over Waldo's, and if he intended to exact it, tomorrow morning might be the last opportunity. So that evening he slipped off to the drugstore and bought a Big Chief tablet and a number two pencil and an envelope and a stamp, and late that night, sitting on the edge of his bed with the naked lightbulb dangling above him like an inspiration, he wrote a sort of valentine:

Last Will & Testimate I Clarence Fronk leave all my wordly goods to Mrs. J. T. Mooney on Railroad St. in Limestone. Sined Clarence M. Fronk Feb 14 1948

Finch folded the paper carefully and put it in the envelope, along with his little bankbook showing that, with interest, there was $826.34 in the account. He sealed the envelope and addressed it to Mrs. Mooney (eight hundred and twenty-six smackers, he reflected, would buy a lot of pork), and as he stamped it and laid it aside, a kind of serenity descended upon him. He allowed himself a few scant moments to enjoy it, and then he turned out the light and took himself to bed, went to sleep without thought, and slept without dreams.

Promptly at six-thirty in the morning, Finch awoke refreshed, dressed himself, and went out into the foggy, bone-

155

chilling dark of the morning, dropping the envelope in the mailbox as he passed the post office. ("He left it all to that old two-dollar flat-back, the little pansy!" Claude would be heard to howl a few days later. "And never done jack-shit for his own goddamn loved ones!") Finch felt light-headed and strangely elated, as though some great and wonderful occasion were impending—the way he used to feel when he was on his way to Brownie's of a Saturday morning. He noted a faint intimation of pressure blooming in his breast, but there was more in it of vengeful exultation than there was of pain or dread.

Finch's bus was always the first out on the morning run, because he had a nine-mile drive up the county highway before he turned off onto the river road and picked up Harry Tom Powers, his first passenger—the same Harry Tom who'd administered Finch's baptism by buttermilk, five dismal years ago. After Harry Tom were the two Barley boys, who shared a congenital predisposition for motion sickness and regularly left Finch a token of their esteem between the seats. Then came, in rapid succession, untold numbers of Brattons, Creeches, Patmores, and Foosneckers, the girls all screechy little harpies, the boys pint-sized assassins, spitball terrorists.

Finch hated them each and every one, equally and unequivocally.

———

Or so he assures himself as he pilots the bus through the darkened streets of Needmore. At the city limits, shifting into high, he feels the pressure tighten its grip around his heart and the first sharp stitch of pain, an ice pick between the ribs. Finch welcomes it and pushes on steadfastly into the darkest hour before the dawn.

After the Foosneckers, the next pickup will be the Kinchlow girl, a blue-eyed blonde whose sweet-sixteen beauty has sometimes set off a certain stirring of the blood even in Finch's own meager loins—but whose misfortune it is to be the daughter of the very Kinchlow who'd robbed Finch of his milk cow, back when the world was young. And so of course she has to go—as do the Pennister boys, who come next, and the Gibbses, and Geezer Wirtschaffner's grandson Johnnie Buckles, and, finally, Buster's nasty little brood. Then will come the long downgrade, and the river.

The county highway snakes along the piney ridges north of town, now and then breaking into the open to reveal the eastern horizon limned by the first pale hint of daybreak. At the Zion Crossroads, where Maudie's old church stands lonely sentinel, Finch takes inventory of his symptoms and determines that his condition is progressing satisfactorily: there's an aching, iron band of pressure around his upper body, like a bruise so deep it goes clear through; he's sick at his stomach, sick as a poisoned crow; his breath is coming hard and fast and short; his puny little arms weigh forty pounds apiece and ache right to the fingertips. And although it's brutally cold inside the bus, his longhandle underwear is drenched with sweat; he's ablaze with fever, yet he's shivering violently, as though someone were walking on his grave.

When you need mercy, importunes a small, familiar voice at his right ear, *be merciful! Take pity! Take pity!*

Finch presses on, clinging grimly to the wheel like a sea captain in a heavy gale, as though he were trying to outdistance his tiny counselor's exhortations. But when he swings off onto the river road, the admonition is still with him, a faint hope striving desperately to make itself come true: *When you need mercy* . . .

The old Powers place, a huge, dilapidated frame farmhouse at the top of the first rise, immediately looms into view above the fog. Finch can see the yellow light of a coal oil lamp in the kitchen window and, as he urges his bus on up the grade, the shadowy, hulking shape of Harry Tom lumbering across the front yard toward the roadside. By the time the bus tops the rise, Harry Tom is standing by the mailbox, yawning hugely in the headlights. Finch downshifts for the stop, and his foot is already poised above the brake, when—

Be merciful! implores the voice. *Take pity!*

Suddenly—he couldn't say why for all the Mrs. Mooneys in the history of the world—Finch pops the clutch and floors the accelerator; the bus slews crazily, spewing mud and gravel; fighting the wheel, he somehow finds the strength to keep it on the road; it rights itself and roars past Harry Tom, his yawn now a gaping oval of astonishment.

Take pity! Take pity!

Finch rushes on into the darkness, the gathering dawn at his back. A few hundred yards down the road the bus plunges headlong into a pocket of fog so dense that he can only steer by memory and instinct, but he doesn't falter; moments later he breaks into the clear again, his foot still mashing the accelerator to the floorboard. Amazingly, even in that brief interval the night has been lifted just a little by the advancing wedge of daylight. The Barley boys float swiftly past the windshield, their faces twin balloons wearing identical stunned expressions. Finch's heart labors mightily, and the pain in his little bosom is colossal, yet Finch himself seems to hover just above it, weightless as a jockey on a sprinting race-horse. The old bus gains speed, slipping and slewing, floundering perilously through the curves. Other faces flash by as fast as fence posts, Brattons and Creeches and Patmores and Foosneckers all slack-jawed and agog, the angel Kinchlow like a roadside statue of the Saint of the Wayfaring Stranger, indiscriminately blessing whoever happens by.

And with each passing face, Finch feels his burden of bitterness and melancholy lifting from him, giving way to something that almost partakes of joy, just as the night gives way to dawn.

There go the Pennisters—four gangling scarecrow silhouettes loping across the front yard, vainly waving their skinny arms—there go the Gibbses, there goes Little Johnny Buckles, bug-eyed as a tree frog.

Meanwhile, three-quarters of a mile down the road from the onrushing bus, Buster Craycraft, having survived yet another night of connubial bliss in the arms of the divine Iota, groggily climbs behind the wheel of the dead wagon, pursuant to an early-morning engagement with a none-too-recently deceased mule over in Toomes County. Iota has succeeded in driving his children—his and Chick Greevey's children—out of the house to meet the bus; they're assembled in a restless little knot beside the road, entertaining themselves by bashing one another over the head with lunch boxes and schoolbooks. The two boys, Clabber and Clawvern, have already reduced all three girls—Claudia, Claudette, and Claudine—to tears of pain and outrage; Clawvern is evidently attempting to make a croquet post of

Baby Claudine by hammering her into the front yard with his geography text.

Buster, lowering his window, maneuvers the dead wagon out of the barn lot onto the roadway. "Hey, shit-heel!" he yells at Clawvern as he passes before the house. "If you don't cut that out, I'm gonna peel your ass when I get home!"

And if Buster hadn't glanced up the road at just that moment, those could've been the last words he ever spoke. Because here comes Uncle Finch's school bus careering round the curve below the house, headlights like owl's eyes in the morning gloom, highballing right straight up the middle of the road as though Buster and the dead wagon weren't there. Buster instinctively slam-shifts into bulldog and stomps on the accelerator, and takes the dead wagon directly to the ditch, as the school bus barrels past it on the left.

For a fraction of a fraction of a second, Buster and Finch look full into each other's face, no more than a yard apart. ("He was white as a onion!" Buster will testify later at the coroner's inquest. "And you coulda knocked his eyeballs off with a broomstick!") Then the unpeopled windows of the bus flick past like empty picture frames, the dead wagon comes to rest in the ditch, and Buster leans out his window and looks back in time to see the rear end of the school bus fishtail crazily in the road, scattering Clawvern and the rest of Iota's flock like barnyard fowl.

But Finch's wheels somehow find the graveled ruts again all by themselves—for the ghastly face that Buster saw was already the face of a corpse, and there is a dead hand at the tiller, and a dead man's foot still jamming the accelerator to the floorboards—and in the blink of an eye the bus has dropped over the brow of the hill and disappeared down the long grade toward the river, even as Finch—*our* Finch, not that poor dead thing at the wheel—is borne aloft by a cloud of tiny golden birds crying, in a thousand thousand sweet discordant little voices, *Per-chick-o-ree! Per-chick-o-reeee! Take pity! Take pity!*

From the hilltop, the Yonder valley spreads itself tremendously, bathed in wan, pellucid light; the swollen river, clotted with black, undulating mats of drift, waits below, shreds of fog rising ghostlike from its gloomy waters.

Finch watches from a great height as the bus, freewheeling now, riding the ruts, galumphs almost joyously down the slope toward its destiny, comically waggling its plump behind as it waddles along from shoulder to shoulder, a jolly cartoon jelly bean of a school bus, like something he and Brownie might have seen one Saturday in the selected short subjects at the Opera House. Entering the curve at the bottom of the hill, with one last boompsadaisy flounce the bus parts company with the road and tumbles end over end down the brushy riverbank and plunges with a mighty cartoon splash into the river. In a heartbeat the murky yellow waters have closed over it, as though it had never been.

Per-chick-o-ree! Per-chick-o-reeeee!

Exulting gloriously, our hero soars up and up into the breaking day. He'll be meeting Brownie soon, on some far distant shore. They're going fishing.